# moonlit dreams
## Laura Muir

an erotic romance

**MOONLIT DREAMS**

Copyright ©2005 by Magic Carpet Books, Inc.

All Rights Reserved

No part of this book may be reproduced,
stored in a retrieval system, or transmitted in any form,
by any means, including mechanical, electronic,
photocopying, recording or otherwise, without
prior written permission from the publisher and author.

First Magic Carpet Books, Inc. edition April 2005

Published in 2005

Manufactured in the United States of America
Published by Magic Carpet Books, Inc.

Magic Carpet Books, Inc.
PO Box 473
New Milford, CT 06776

Library of Congress Cataloging in Publication Date

Moonlit Dreams by Laura Muir
$9.95

ISBN# 0-9755331-8-5

Book Design: P. Ruggieri

# MOONLIT DREAMS

### Laura Muir

# PART ONE

# Chapter One

*From sea to shining sea...*

E lizabeth kept hearing this phrase all night in her sleep, tossing from side to side, her body the curl of a comma between the line's constant repetition. *From sea to shining sea...* She turned over, grasping her pillow like a floating object in the dark depths of her unconscious, part of her detached from her movement like the calm gaze of a mermaid looking on... *From sea to shining sea...* She turned onto her other side again... Finally, the crack of golden light between her white curtains ended the night-long statement with its exclamation mark on her eyelids, and she awoke.

The shape of the North American continent as seen from space had accompanied the endlessly repeating phrase that crossed her mind all night like a train with its linked cars of words. The sentence went from one shore to the other as she tossed back and forth, the oceans on each side of her continent-sized bed a translucent blue rippling with silver highlights like a wrinkled satin shirt. The different cities were marked by colorful gems, transforming America into a shining golden brooch over the vast heart beating behind the darkness of space. Elizabeth was twenty-nine-years-old, and it was only now she felt she had a real grip on her life, as if time in passing had become a rein she could grasp and mysteriously control herself with. It was quite a task to avoid the conventional pits in her positive path, but the force of desire she had always possessed made her leap over the emptiness of each passing day as she searched for someone – a man – with her same lust for life. The sun was an infinitely valuable coin forged for the exchange of their desires, if she could only find him. When she at last met him, they would be able to buy whatever dreams they could conceive of, tethering the beautiful horses of their creative energy at the crossroad of time and space as they enjoyed the intoxicating warmth of their spirits poured into the fragile vessels of their flesh which they would passionately shatter in the end...

Elizabeth smiled at these images, pleased she had remembered to turn on her Dream Recorder last night. She got out of bed and turned a black knob on the wall all the way to the right, extinguishing the colors in her room. The walls and dresser became clear panels again as she strolled languidly into the bathroom because it was Saturday and school was closed. She saw herself enter through a mirror on the shower door and paused. Catching sight of herself was always a pleasant shock. She had intense dark-brown eyes and hair that waved softly down to her waist, her lips were ancient Egyptian in their fullness and her figure was slender but curving, her small breasts as perfectly rounded as a classical statue's.

Just as she turned the hot water on in the tub the phone rang in the living room. She quickly slipped into a short white house dress and ran to answer it.

A luminous twelve-inch-tall tall figure appeared on the black stage in front of the vertical dialing panel. She stood with her arms crossed, knowing that was how she appeared in his living room now. 'Hello,' she said politely, because she didn't really know the caller. She had met him briefly at the school when he dropped off his little brother, and it annoyed her that he had gotten her number.

'Good morning, Elizabeth. How are you?'

'Fine.' She yawned discreetly. 'Are you calling about your brother? He's doing very well in class.'

'No, actually, I was just wondering if you were doing anything tonight.'

She saw him glance down and knew he was studying her shining bare legs, and probably wishing he could lay her small figure in the palm of his hands.

'Thank you, John, but I have plans.'

'Then how about tomorrow night?'

She glanced at the fly swatter on one of her window sills but new that, unfortunately, his luminous atoms were invulnerable to it. 'I'm sorry, John, but I really don't think so. Thank you any way and have a great day.' She switched off the receiver, relieved to watch him instantly sucked down into the platform's porous black cells that resembled the honey cones of a beehive. She was pleased he had called before her shower so she could wash off the feel of him, but then she exclaimed beneath her breath when she saw the pile of exams on her glass coffee table waiting to be graded. Fortunately, she had the whole weekend to inhale an illusion of freedom before she dove back into the aquarium of routine on Monday, swimming placidly back and forth between home and work. Finally in the shower, she wondered again how she had ended up as a teacher of ancient history in a private school for boys. At least she enjoyed her job. It also served to keep her more base desires in check through the same principal that operates in a vaccine – every day she was injected with fresh, milling germs of temptation which made her even more immune than she naturally was to sex without love. Her student's ages ranged from thirteen to eighteen. Elizabeth often felt as smugly hungry and dangerously without scruples as a cat enclosed in a room with a horde of delicious mice dressed in pure white shirts. It amused her that they often didn't listen to a word she said. They glanced at each other and smiled surreptitiously, quickly picking up their pens in a pretense of note-taking whenever she paused in her lecture and swept her gaze like the beam of a lighthouse over their emotionally turbulent forms. Yet she loved their waves of mischievousness and the shining spray of their laughter. She could almost see the shifting currents of their thoughts, and distinctly feel the undertow of their innocently strong desire for her.

She had her favorite student, of course. She did her absolute best to conceal it, but it was all she could do to keep herself from caressing the soft blonde hair resting on the tender nape of his neck as he bent over an exam. For her he was the beautiful, sensitive heart of the student body, the other boys mingling anonymously as cells most of the time as far as her awareness of them was concerned. It gave her such pleasure to look directly at Michael as she said something in order to experience the subtle pleasure of his reaction, placing the pressure of her mind on his veins and striking the responsive chords of his feelings. The school where she taught had been founded nine years ago by a poet named Jim Grant. He was thirty-six and had made a fortune as the singer of a successful rock band. His desire was to catch young men when they were old enough to think for themselves and enable them to do so, as opposed to saddling them with concepts designed to break their spirits so that society could safely rein than in at graduation. He felt a teacher should be like a bareback rider, not burdening students with centuries of intellectual sorrow or digging in the rigid spurs of rational thought while at the same time not letting them wildly throw off an education. Jim provided the school's students with the adventurously appealing image of the teacher as journeying with them through an open field of ideas; unconsciously suggesting that knowledge will enable them to get the most out of their spontaneity like a rider skillfully driving a powerful motorcycle. Jim was their beloved principal, and it was a constant source of annoyance to Elizabeth that she didn't love him.

She stepped out of the shower. There wasn't a day she didn't wonder about Jim; he had become a natural part of her thought processes. There was no doubt about the fact that she desired him, and she thought of him now as she dried herself off slowly...

She thought of his softly waving shoulder-length brown hair; his eyes black as coals shining with the mysterious heat of his inner life; his hands with their strong, sensitive fingers between which a cigarette always hung with a limp air of burning submission to him, evoking the way a woman must feel when she was in his arms; his perfectly curving lips lying beneath his black eyes' penetrating gaze like a soft bed in an eternal night, centuries of human history flickering in procession through his thoughts; his slender body and strong, relaxed shoulders the noble form of the technological world, his lean sensuality possible only when food is abundant. She enjoyed remembering how he had made it perfectly clear, more than once, that he desired her, too.

*But he doesn't love me*, she thought. *He desires any beautiful woman he meets, and he has at least three girl friends that I know of at the moment.*

She slipped into a fresh house dress and started making herself some breakfast – coffee and toast and scrambled eggs to give her energy to tackle the pile of exams awaiting her.

*Maybe that's why we're such good friends, because we haven't yet burned out our sensual connection.*

She discarded this cynical notion, regarding it distastefully, like a piece of pollution washed up on the essentially pure waves of her profoundly positive view of life. 'Why don't I love him?' she asked herself out loud. 'I like him more than anyone else I know. I guess I *would* love him if he wasn't such a hopeless womanizer.'

The phone rang again and she walked towards it suspiciously. 'That better not be John thinking he gets three strikes before he's out.' Reluctantly, she pressed the receiver button.

'What up, sweetheart?' Jim was surrounded by a decidedly not enchanted mist of cigarette smoke. He was wearing his eternal black leather pants and an attractively cut black velvet suit jacket over a black T-shirt.

'Jim... Hi... You look dressed for a serious night out.'

'Where do you want to go?'

She laughed. 'It's only ten o'clock in the morning.'

'Yes, but I'm going over to the school now to finish up some things and I'll probably be there until six, so I'll drive straight to your place. You have nine hours to decide what you want to eat tonight.'

She laughed again and was about to say something, but he was already gone. 'This isn't fair,' she mumbled, staring into the empty black honey cones of the phone's stage where he had just stood. 'I'm being tested!' She fell onto her couch and stared helplessly before her, a hurricane of conflicting emotions suddenly raging inside her. The frail bud of her conscious assertion that she could not love him was easily destroyed by a flood of desire she couldn't help feel was negative, because it left her soul's conceptual structure shattered in its wake. She stared at her thighs emerging from the soft white cloth of her dress and thought about the famous guitarist whose image matched that of the dream man who had lived inside her since she was a girl. It occurred to her that his group had traveled from shore to shore as often as the phrase in her dream last night. She had read in a magazine somewhere that he had recently moved down to Coral Beach, and the idea that it might be possible to meet him suddenly beat on her mind's door with a haunting urgency.

# Chapter Two

A melodic string of bells cascaded across the ceiling, communicating their shivering excitement to Elizabeth as she nervously caressed her black silk dress and ran to open the door.

'This is our anniversary,' Jim announced, standing formally on the threshold. 'One year ago today, I became your boss.'

'Oh, that's right,' she exclaimed, and mentally slapped herself for feeling disappointed, she turned away. She heard him close the door and turned to face him again. He was standing before her black couch. 'We've known each other over a year and you've never been here,' she observed, smiling and trying to sound casual.

'That's because it's hard enough to resist you in a professional environment, not to mention when there's a bedroom six feet away.' He looked down and she realized she had unconsciously placed her glass coffee table between them. 'What am I supposed to do with this?' he asked in his usual soft, contemplative voice. 'Shatter it into star-like pieces in my overwhelming desire to possess you?'

'Sure,' she said, and waited.

He shrugged and looked around him. 'Nice place.'

'Where are we going?' she asked, a little annoyed.

'I asked you to decide that and gave you nine long hours in

which to do so.' He moved over to her wall-to-wall bookshelf and studied her selection.

'I rarely eat out, so how should I know what's a nice place? You're the one who has a different date every night and have lived here for years.'

He turned to her CD and DVD collection, the relaxed flow of his movements showing her that he was unhurt by her remark's cutting edge. 'You didn't tell me you were an artist, Elizabeth.' He had come upon her wall of paintings, and the genuine surprise and pleasure in his voice drew her to him like a magnet. She stood beside him and saw her work again for the first time through his eyes. 'Why didn't you tell me?' he demanded.

'Because, they're nothing...'

'What the hell do you mean they're *nothing*?'

She felt beautiful and helpless as a butterfly pinned beneath his sharp stare. He was so close she almost felt the warm caress of his breath blowing all the words out of her mind like dandelion seeds and leaving her only with the wish that he would kiss her. 'I have a definite vision, but I'm not an artist,' she tried to explain. 'I learned to draw the human figure from comic books, and I use magic markers and oil pastels and crayons and regular writing pens, so they're not really paintings. I think of them as metaphysical cartoons.'

He laughed. 'That's exactly what they are and they're wonderful.' He was looking at a nude man and woman on a beach. She was lying on top of him, her black hair flowing over his face, his golden head visible beneath it. Their arms and legs were spread wide so they were the same shape as the red starfish scattered around them. The blue-white sand reflected the full moon cutting a silver path across the dark-green ocean glittering with the golden spray of cresting waves.

There were eight other pictures and Jim examined each one for about two minutes. By the time he was finished, Elizabeth was leaning heavily against him. 'Do you like them?' she asked weakly, and his arm slipped around her waist like the curve of a comma deliciously separating the past moment from the next, when she knew he would turn her to him and kiss her... but he didn't. She closed her eyes, slipping her arms around his neck to rest her head on his shoulder, and she felt all the connections of her thoughts fall apart and her mind shut off like a light in the warm darkness of his embrace.

'Shall we go eat?' she heard him ask before his tongue began tasting hers hungrily and she pulled away, eager to bite his warm neck, thriving on his quiet moans and the way he clutched the elusive black silk of her dress as if his life depended on it. She gasped as his hand slipped between her legs, curving like a cobra's hood from the hard length of his arm, his eyes flashing into hers, the intensity of his feeling weakening her like venom. One of his fingers slid easily beneath her soft cotton panty and she shook her head, ridding herself of remaining objections as he gently stabbed her with it, killing any willpower she still possessed to resist him. Her body grew limp but he held her up with his free arm. His finger stirring up her pussy juices was like a twister's slender but devastating force causing disconnected images to fly behind her closed eyelids – her favorite student staring at her very seriously... the musician she always daydreamed about strumming his guitar... Jim smoking at his desk followed by his string of girl friends like a chain around his neck from which the earth hung heavily...

She pushed him away.

He stared at her for a moment, then smiled softly and took her arm. 'Shall we?'

# Chapter Three

Thoughts raced through Elizabeth's head as fast as the colors of the twilight rushed by outside Jim's black Corvette. She had no idea where they were going just as she could come to no conclusion about their possible future together. *I'm not about to become another link in his sensual chain, or another column in the profane temple of his conquests.* She desperately sought to ignore the silent scream burning like poison in her blood – he doesn't love me any more than the others, he doesn't love me! Then she realized they were headed for the ocean and for some reason this made her feel better.

Night had fallen by the time she heard distant waves murmuring a secret answer to the motor's purring. He pulled into a sand parking lot in which the few scattered cars gleamed like huge polished seashells beneath his headlights' golden wave, and through the corner of her eye she saw the quick, supple twist of his wrist as he switched them off, plunging them into darkness.

'There aren't any streetlights out here?' she asked a little nervously.

'Enjoy the mystery,' he whispered.

Elizabeth felt his presence beside her more intensely than if she could see him, and she distinctly heard the ocean now like a slumbering, but unfathomably powerful being. As she listened, concentrating on what Jim was going to do, the water's muted roar blended with the magnified sound of their own breathing in the car's small shell, and her heart started beating as hard as the waves on the shore.

'Ready?' he asked.

'Yes...' She let herself out of the car and stood overpowered by the embrace of wind and darkness until Jim came around and gently took her arm. He led her confidently across the sand, supporting her as she struggled to keep her balance in her high-heeled sandals. At the time time she surrendered to a stimulating sense of unreality; wonderfully, languidly, possessed by Jim's fearless stride. She saw two gilded wooden doors appear in the distance and was almost certain she was creating them with her imagination. Torches in black sconces burned on either side of them, crackling passionately and a little angrily beneath the relentless teasing of the sea breeze. 'Is this for real?' she asked, glancing at her companion.

His silence was answer and reprimand at once, his eyes cool and deep as the night holding hers. The shadows from the moving flames flickered across his features so they seemed to speak to her silently, telling her that desire's invisible power is the only thing that's real.

The doors slowly opened at their approach and she saw red lights pulsing in the dark interior, so that for a moment she suffered the impression they were the exposed hearts of the people dining inside. Pausing uncertainly on the threshold, she saw a blue beam of light coursing swiftly through the room and illuminating different faces in its blood-like flow between the small round tables evocative of white blood cells. She couldn't tell where this light was coming from or where it was headed; it seemed to be everywhere at once. As it passed over the red lamps, it washed the tablecloths violet and made the whole place look as if it was under water. Without waiting for the hostess, Jim led her to a table and suddenly she remembered his finger inside her, stirring up dreamy ideas, and she felt wonderfully relaxed and open when he offered her a chair beside a glass wall. The sand outside was rhythmically washed by red, blue and violet waves, an impenetrable darkness threatening just a few feet beyond them.

'Oh, Jim!' she sighed. 'I love your taste in restaurants.'

'That's not all you love about me.'

A young man in black jeans and a black T-shirt handed them two faux golden menus, smiled, and strolled away.

Elizabeth began studying the selection, but Jim put his menu down and sat looking at her in such a way that she couldn't concentrate, especially now that she knew how good his lips and tongue tasted. She set the menu down carefully, certain he noticed her hand was trembling slightly. 'I'll have the lobster,' she declared and stared down at the red lamp between them, only to find herself imagining his naked body washed by the soft blue light flowing around the room. She met his eyes and smiled faintly, the flicker of a new feeling between them that might become a sublime fire or sadly burn only a few hot nights before dying in the tepid ashes of their professional circumstances.

The waiter returned. Jim ordered lobster for both of them and a bottle of Italian *Pinot Grigio*. Then he offered her a cigarette and she shook her head. That was another thing she didn't like about him – his cigarettes and his women were as numerous and common.

'Isn't it amazing how everyone is a unique being even though the majority of people haven't consciously done anything to deserve this honor?' he asked conversationally.

'Yes!' She laughed.

'So, why aren't you in love with me?'

It took her a moment to recover from the exquisite experience of his stabbing directness. 'Because I'm not the harem type. I could never share you with other women.'

'Who says you'd have to?'

'That's just the way you're made, Jim.'

He intently killed his half smoked cigarette in the clear crystal ashtray, and the unexpected sadness in his eyes gripped her throat like hands.

'For me faithfulness is of profound, even metaphysical, importance,' she tried to explain. 'I mean, I guess I have fairy-tale feelings about it, in a way, but I really believe the world is created by love... that men and women possess polar energies that interact and create time and space... I mean, it's hard to put into words, and it's not as simple as woman being the earth and man the heavens... woman being deep, dark, wet soil, and man intense, direct light... yet, I feel there is something to that, it's not just poetic imagery; it's somehow reflected in our different emotional natures. But we're not at the school, so I won't lecture.'

'I like it when you lecture me. You should do it more often... Elizabeth, until I met you I had never really been able to talk to a woman. I could only express a part of myself with them because I knew they wouldn't be able to handle the rest of me; that they wouldn't understand what I was saying. It's different with you.'

'Well, that's how I feel about men. I've never met anyone I can really talk to either.'

Their food arrived and at the sight of the large red lobsters they smiled at each other. Elizabeth was exhilarated as she cracked the crustacean's hot armor. In a similar way the cool shell of their professional friendship was being shattered into a delicious intimacy. They concentrated on the tender white meat for a while, smiling over the rim of their wine glasses. Her awareness gradually began arching euphorically over everything, past and future two pots of gold on either side of the rainbow-colored present. Jim's smile as he chewed beneath his serious black eyes made her feel as if the small round table was the whole world which belonged exclusively to them, his throat reddened by the lamp pulsing gently as he finished another glass of wine like a heart absorbing a divine spirit.

'I always got along with my mother,' she heard him saying.

'I was disappointed with my father. I could talk to my mom about everything and she always understood, even if she didn't agree, and I knew she always loved me even when I drove her crazy.'

She smiled at him indulgently.

'I guess she knew from the beginning that I would give her hell,' he went on. 'I refused to walk for a long time. I guess I just didn't feel like it. So, one day, she put all my favorite toys on one end of the rug, sat me down on the other, and she encouraged me to walk over towards them. I looked at her, looked at the toys, looked down at the rug, and then, staring at her, I just pulled on the rug and brought the toys over to me. She was never able to trick me.' He laughed to himself as he refilled her glass. 'When I was five, I told her I was going to run away from home, and she said to go ahead and have a nice time, and I told her that using reverse psychology on me wasn't going to work, that I was still leaving. She ran into her room and cried all afternoon.'

'You used the term "reverse psychology" on her when you were five?' Elizabeth was delighted. 'What a cute little brat you must have been.'

'Actually, I was fat, and most of the kids in school hated me because I was a brain. I read all the time, and kids tend to hate you when you always have your arm up, eager to give your answer to everything. I suppose that's true even of people when they grow up.' He lit another cigarette. 'When I was nine, I started getting worried about death. At first I was really into science, but then I realized it couldn't account for everything. I didn't actually put it to myself this way, but I knew empirical knowledge couldn't account for the feeling in life, for the mysterious energy of our actions, of our aspirations... of love.'

'I know.' She stared down at her wine as if seeing her own past in its inspiring clarity. 'I feel like I went through my midlife crisis at twenty. That's when the reality of death hit me, and its haunting contrast to love's undying power... True sensuality is a mysterious, expressive union of your physical reality with the exciting force inside you... which you see in someone you love,' she stammered as though trying to cross a profound, surging river on the inadequate and slippery stones of words.

He stared at her intently a moment, then coolly brought her back onto the steady shore of his memories. 'I know, I went through my mid-life crisis at thirteen. That's when I became hopelessly depressed about the state of the world. I was also seriously into magic. There was no doubt in my mind that I was smart enough to bend objects with my will. I had one friend, and we discovered *The Tibetan Book of the Dead*, not the real one, of course, but it was full of exciting spells and ideas. Then, when I was about fourteen, I joined the track team, and suddenly I lost all my fat and girls started noticing me. Women have been like a drug for me.' He spoke softly, as if to himself. 'At first I was intoxicated by the power I had over them. You see, I discovered that I could talk them into doing anything I wanted them to. They were attracted to me now, and I found it easy as a spider to snare them with words that sounded sincere but which I really made up on the spot. I'd been playing the guitar since I was eight, and I told each girl I'd written that song just for her last night. That was the beginning of my evil period.'

'Which seems not to have ended yet.' She frowned, her elation evaporating.

'Perhaps you're the one destined to kill the spider, Elizabeth.'

'I never kill spiders, it's bad luck... No, thank you, I've had enough wine.' She covered her glass with her hand when he made to refill it.

'Would you like to go into the music room?' he asked abruptly. 'They have life size, 3-D videos in there.'

She thought of the musician she had felt knocking on her heart that morning after Jim called her, and felt it skip a beat as if the bolt of impossibility was suddenly sprung. 'Sure, let's go.'

# Chapter Four

In the music room, Jim ordered another bottle of wine, and Elizabeth walked to the control panel as the song that was playing ended. Luminous blue letters crossed the screen's black space like a train, reminding her of her dream, while the computer searched for the track she desired. Then the darkness reverberated with loud clicking sounds, as if time and space were somehow being reprogrammed, and three shafts of light in the form of a pyramid shot down into the center of the room carrying the band inside them. The drum-set shone and pulsed like a brilliant cluster of red giants and young, blue-hot stars, and it was only after a moment that she dared to look at the guitarist's miraculous, dimensional luminosity in a blood-red jacket contrasting with the glowing golden organ of his instrument. Returning to the table, she passed right next to him feeling as shy as if he was real. His light fingertips flashed like the particles of its current, his unique being energy's latent consciousness.

She resumed her seat and sat spellbound until the song pulled into its final notes, the swirling colors composing the three dimensional image slowing down then abruptly vanishing.

Jim got up. 'I'll be right back.' He disappeared, and suddenly she saw the black-and- silver bar that had been hidden behind his head. A man with blond hair was sitting directly in her line of sight about nine yards away, and she felt that he was resting not on the stool but on the point where her power of vision and her physical sight mysteriously converged. Her pulse fluttered, her mind swayed strangely, her heart beats suddenly heavy stones she was crossing over a vast darkness as his presence threw her completely off balance. Then she was possessed by a thrilling terror when she realized it was the guitarist, in the flesh, staring at her, until the bartender said something to him and he looked away.

*It's impossible that he's here! It's impossible!* She saw the woman sitting next to him appraise the angle of his back and thighs. He turned to her when she touched his arm, and Elizabeth felt herself awkwardly floating in a meaningless void deprived of the gravitational power and center of his attention. She stared at the right angle of his back and thighs in a light-blue jacket and black pants as if they were the shape of, and the reason for, everything... all the street corners she had ever walked and ever would; the corners of all the rooms she had ever been in and of the one she would die in; the vertical buildings and horizontal streets of every city in the world; his breath-filled chest the sky over the deep land of his thighs; his black pants the lanes of a highway on which she imagined herself kneeling, sucking on the eternal mandrake root beneath...

'Would you like to meet him?' Jim was back and looking down at her with the kindly air of a guardian angel.

'You *know* him?' It was a whispered scream.

'Yes. He's planning to send his son to our school.'

She closed her eyes for a second, and when she opened them again they were expressionless – the mechanisms of sight were intact, but the being viewing the images projected onto the mind had lost interest. With a terrible cold detachment, she observed Jim approaching the bar, the guitarist quickly turning away from the woman and smiling, shaking Jim's hand, and then smiling again as he looked her way. Then they were both walking towards her and she saw her hand clutch the glass before her stiff as a bird's claw nervously fighting the urge to fly away.

'Alex, this is Elizabeth, the school's ancient history teacher and my best friend. I believe she knows who you are.'

Alex smiled and offered her his hand. She took it without letting herself feel it, but as he and Jim were seating themselves, the memory of his firm warmth seemed to burn into her palm.

'So how's Linda?' Jim delicately caressed a cigarette between two fingertips while he spoke as if it was the lovingly burning body in question.

'She and Mark are up at her parents' farm for a week. She's teaching him to ride.'

Elizabeth's awareness was hovering over her body like a puppeteer, ready to pull her lips up at the appropriate moment, to lift her glass to her lips at reasonable intervals, and to mouth polite lines when it was her turn to speak. Alex was looking at her, but now she could see another woman swimming happily in the light-blue depth of one of his eyes and a child surfacing in the other, so that his gaze lost its intimate touch. And yet he had been staring at her from the bar...

'How old is Mark now?' Jim was selfishly holding onto her with this painfully civil chain of conversation.

'He's seven.'

*Which means at least eight years of making love to him*, she thought, and at that moment she envied his wife more hopelessly than she had ever feared death. Sipping her water, she followed the narrow, sky-blue path of his tie up to his eyes, beautifully set and shadowed under light-brown eyebrows. His cheeks still possessed the tender fullness of a boy's in an otherwise lean face, his lips undulating enough for her vision to enjoy, but they were too elusively slender for her imagination to taste. His hair fell straight and bright as wheat over his forehead's broad field, but it was softer, almost like light shining over it...

'What are you smiling at like the Cheshire cat, Elizabeth?' Jim asked her abruptly.

'Nothing...' She thought she sounded incredibly stupid.

'Come now, to describe pleasure is another pleasure, so tell us what you were thinking. If I know you, it's worth sharing.'

'I wasn't thinking anything in particular. When I feel good thoughts float by and I smile at them, that's all.'

'Tell us one,' Alex requested.

*Oh, God!* 'Well...' Her eyes fell on his lips and, hypnotically, they became a barge on which she floated, casually fishing out lines. 'I was thinking that since energy is indestructible, the smart thing is not to control our emotions but to concentrate them.'

His smile deepened. 'Another one.'

'I read somewhere once that the poetic word is the only sound allied to silence.' She made herself look into his eyes, and there wasn't anyone in them now except his own being; her soul felt the warm touch of his energy.

'Don't stop,' Jim commanded. 'Keep going until we tell you to.'

Elizabeth felt joyful and beautiful as an Egyptian priestess reclining on the solar bark of Alex's smile. '"As the body rests in its bed, so does the mind in its beliefs".'

'In its "doctrine".' Jim corrected her. 'Swedenborg.'

'Thank you, but don't interrupt her anymore,' Alex requested.

'"A real artist does not worry about who will see his work, for angels look over his shoulder and he creates in their company". Rudolf Steiner. "Art, always a daughter of the divine, has become estranged from her parent".' She concentrated on the flame as Jim lit a cigarette. '"An image of the universe is shaped by forehead and upper head, and an image of experience in circling the sun, is felt artistically in the formation of the eyes. Imagine: the repose of the fixed stars shows in the tranquil vault of brow and upper head, and planetary circling in the mobile gaze of the eye. As for the mouth of man",' her eyes were resting on Alex's again, '"it represents the whole human being as he lives with his soul in his body. The human head mirrors the universe artistically. In forehead and the arching crown of the head we see the still vault of the heavens; in eye, nose and upper lip, planetary movement;

in mouth and chin, a resting within oneself".'

'Enough of Steiner.' Jim cut in. 'Give us some poetry.'

'That sounded pretty poetic to me,' Alex remarked, draining his glass.

'That's the problem, he's supposed to be a philosopher.'

'Shall I go on?' she asked.

'Please,' they both answered at once, then laughed, and Jim took the opportunity to catch the waitress as she passed and order another bottle of wine for them all.

'This quote is from ancient Egypt. "Our first duty is to Ra. Ra decrees that we shall always act out of love; and to act out of love is to be happy. Therefore, it is our duty to be happy".'

'Is this what you're teaching my boys, Elizabeth?' Jim asked. 'Remind me to sit in on one of your classes.'

'Shut up, Jim.' Alex took up her defense again. 'Go on, please.'

'Maybe she's tired.'

'I've just warmed up,' she declared. 'This one's also Egyptian... "Human beings are to animals as the gods are to us. They are different rungs of the ladder between the sand and the stars".'

'Interesting,' Alex murmured.

Jim toasted her, smiling. 'Well done, Elizabeth.'

'I remember a poem now. It's called, *Socket to Me*. Don't laugh, Jim, it's a pun. "It pulls out the plug, but before bulbs, we're illumination. Before stereos, music. Yes, death disconnects, but we remain current". Mario, another teacher at the school, wrote that one.'

'So, what do you think, Alex, do you still want to send Mark to us?'

'More than ever.'

'Elizabeth's an artist.' Jim exhaled a path of red and blue smoke across the table. 'You have to see her work some time, you'd love it. We could even drive over there now, if you're not doing anything.'

*Moonlit Dreams*

Elizabeth stopped breathing.

'I'd love to,' Alex replied.

'Good. You can follow us in your car.'

'I took a cab here.'

'Excellent, you can come with us. She's got a nice place. God knows why, but I only just saw it tonight myself.'

'Shall we?' Alex looked at her, and he and Jim both stood up before she could answer or believe what was happening.

Outside, the night breathed in excited gusts as Elizabeth watched it throw fresh embraces around Alex, tugging at his jacket and passionately caressing his hair. Jim took her right arm as they started across the sand, with Alex walking on her left, and she was afraid the attraction she felt for him would become visible in the complete darkness.

'Here.' Jim released her, moving away, and Alex gently took her hand, slowly guiding her to the passenger's side. She got into the car conscious only of one fact – that he was in the seat behind hers. Jim shifted gears and backed out, saying, 'I guess you can separate people into two main categories – those who are always asking "what if" and those who only say "so what"?'

They all laughed.

'A lot of "what ifs" have gone through my head tonight.'

'Such as?' Alex sounded perfectly relaxed.

A black cat shot across the road, forcing Jim to brake suddenly before they could continue on their way. 'That's it. A "what if" is like a black cat crossing your path. It can either be loving and beautiful, or it'll scratch your eyes out and so much for the romantic vision.'

She more felt Alex's laughter than heard it.

'"Piano keys are marble slabs and black coffins",' she quoted. '"Our bodies rise and fall between heaven and earth like fingers on different notes".'

'Jesus, who wrote *that*?'

She hesitated, unable to decipher Jim's tone. 'I did,' she admitted.

He laughed, and no one spoke for the rest of the drive, until

Jim announced, 'We're here, but I'm suddenly seriously tired. I'm afraid you'll have to take another cab home later, Alex, if you survive her body of work, that is.'

'I don't mind.' Alex spoke lightly.

She felt Jim knew exactly how she felt and she only dared to glance at him as she opened the car door. His eyes held hers intently as his understanding of all she was feeling mysteriously penetrated her. Her heart beat wildly, like fists trying to push him away even as she wished desperately that he would stay.

'Good night, Elizabeth,' he said. 'Sweet dreams.'

# Chapter Five

When Elizabeth stepped into her dark apartment it felt strangely cold and lifeless, like an empty seashell. She was outside its solid safety, vulnerably floating in the power of her imagination as the guitarist's blood beat on his heart's shore impossibly close to hers. So many pleasurable daydreams of him had flowed lightly around her reason that his actual presence made her feel awkward as a beached mermaid, with no hope of ever returning to the enchanted realm of her fantasies now that she knew he was responsible for a family. The fact that he had a wife tasted like dry sand as she switched on the overhead light and clung to the familiar objects of her living room to keep her feelings from plunging dangerously into his blue eyes.

'My drawings are over there.' She lifted her arm slightly, like a bird's maimed wing. 'I'll be right back.' She flew away into her bathroom.

An unexpectedly beautiful and flushed face greeted her in the mirror, wide open brown eyes staring back at her with the powerful blankness of a frightened doe. 'I hate you, Jim! I hate you for this!' she hissed. Yet a moment later she felt grateful to him, the blind tears she had shed now glistening a fresh dew of positivism in her head. Whatever happened, at least it was real!

Alex was lying across her bed when she emerged, his head

resting unconcerned in his hands as he gazed at her large viewing screen. He looked at her when she appeared. 'I'd rather see some of your dreams instead,' he said.

'All right...'

'Do you have one with me in it?' He smiled.

'The question is whether I have one without you in it,' she confessed before she could stop herself.

He didn't appear surprised. He simply stared back at the screen, waiting.

She had no idea what dream she could possibly show him, and was desperately wondering where she was going to sit. Then, suddenly, the whole night seemed so impossible that she just shrugged and walked over to her DVD rack, each sleeve neatly marked with dates and titles in red.

'Let's get some colors in here, Elizabeth,' Alex demanded pleasantly.

'Yes, sir.' His forcefulness pleased her. She grasped the black knob and turned to him as if to her class from the chalkboard. 'What colors would you like?' she asked like a waitress taking his order.

'Violet for the walls...'

She obeyed him, very pleased with his choice.

'Lighter, that's a bit too purple... there. Now, please make the doors green...'

'Green?'

'Yes, a dark forest green.'

She did as he said.

'And your dresser should be golden... wonderful. Now you can turn off the light.'

'Not until I put the dream in...' She attempted to examine their titles again, but her nerves were like piranhas turning her red cursive into a blood-like stream she couldn't make head or tail of. She felt like a specter standing by its own grave – her dream shelf containing all her desires and fantasies – in a haunting afterlife, her god fallen before her. 'I can't...' she said helplessly.

'Why not?'

'Because... '

'Why, Elizabeth?' Stretched out on the flowing blue comforter of her bed, his body and golden head were like a warm, sunlit island, and she was a miserably disembodied soul, his wife the weapon still killing her. 'The sooner you stop thinking you're embarrassed,' he went on, 'the sooner you can come here.' He rested his left hand on the bed beside him – the beautifully sensitive spider that had spun so many magical combinations of notes and captured her in the sensual web of his songs.

She closed her eyes, her conscience blinking off for a moment under a terrible surge of desire. Leaving it to fate, she grabbed a DVD at random, fed it to the machine's crouching black shape, and switched off the light. The walls of her bedroom shone flawless as the heart of a crystal around them as she crawled up from the end of the bed towards him like a black cat in her clinging dress. 'Here,' she whispered, propping two pillows up comfortably behind him.

He pulled her down so her head rested comfortably on his shoulder and her mind became purely blank, reflecting the large, luminous projection screen before them, the soft clicking and whirring of the Dream Recorder replacing the mechanisms of thought. She relaxed completely, conscious only of Alex's warmth and the slow rise and fall of his chest, its gentle rhythm echoing the beginnings of life in the ocean's sun-warmed depths.

The screen's white light dimmed into a slowly swirling mist, the straight, slender trunks of trees piercing it as they followed her dream over a winding dirt path swift as a snake. Then the scene changed to a darkened room. Through glass doors lay the forest, and silhouetted against it were the curving bodies of guitars resting in the arms of their stands. Alex was sitting in the room, another guitar idle in his lap as he gazed outside. The dawn's soft light struck his face so that his features seemed to grow out of the darkness from his heart's mysteriously infinite seed. She was out there somewhere, the mist her clinging dress, the thick brown earth a soft avalanche of hair over her bare shoulders' ivory treasures, the delicate veins of all the forest leaves beneath her skin...

The scene changed to her running between the trees with the speed and ease of light glinting off dew. She paused at a leaf where a caterpillar arched up to greet her slender finger, then ran on, heading towards the shining diamond-shaped pane of his window fastening the rippling green forest around it like a cloak. Her dress vanished beneath the sun's caress as she heard the notes of his guitar and flew on their path unhindered, breathlessly fast, until she reached the small clearing where his house stood. She hid behind trees, stealing glances into the dark room at his golden head bent over his instrument, shyly approaching the glass door. He looked up and she flew to the side of the house, but he began calling to her with high, plaintive notes she couldn't resist as she clung like a spider to the oak walls. His notes became small screams, escalating urgently, until she pressed her naked body against the glass...

The screen went black, marking the moment she awoke and the dream ended.

'Oh, no,' Alex moaned.

Another dream began, but by now Elizabeth could hardly concentrate. She stared fixedly into the darkness beyond his chest, her bedroom walls resembling a violet mist, anxiously controlling her hand as it longed to exert its own will. It was lying on his chest playing dead, but she wouldn't be able to command it much longer, even though she tried using cutting, whip-sharp thoughts to stop it – he's married, he has a child, he doesn't care about you at all, you'll never see him again after tonight. These thoughts burned painfully into her heart, but they had no effect on the force of the desire intensifying inside her. His warmth traveled down the paths of her fingers to her heart's castle, where it easily defeated all her rational defenses, and from there it journeyed to every other part of her body like an urgent message proclaimed throughout a kingdom. HE'S ALL THAT MATTERS she saw in gilded letters the shape of stems and leaves punctuated with red flowers, and allowed the will freezing her hand to melt so she could caress his chest.

*He's letting me*, she thought giddily. She followed the trail of his buttons, plucking them up and tossing them away like wishing stones, her desire coming true as she slipped her hand beneath his shirt's soft cotton. Pleasure buds gently burst in all her nerve ends as her fingertips came in contact with the grassy roughness of his hair. He lay perfectly still and the world was suspended for her. Her restless hand wanted to travel south to the hot realm rich with hurricanes of sensation, but she didn't have permission to cross his belt's magical border. So her fingers adventured cautiously north, lightly caressing his neck as if it was a sacred column joining the heaven and earth of his mind and body.

He brought her hand up to his lips, resting them for a moment at the center of her lifelines, then his tongue followed her fingers up to gently bite their soft round ends. Fire quivered down the center of her body in response to the hot tip of his tongue licking her skin. He rested her hand back on his chest and slowly guided it down before abandoning it to reach up and stroke her long hair.

The images of a dream flashing behind her, Elizabeth knelt over him, meeting his eyes. She didn't expect him to grasp the depth of what she was feeling, only the wordless truth that she would always care for him as she unbuckled his belt and then removed his black pants and underwear. He had already kicked off his shoes before spreading himself across her bed, and he helped her now by lifting his hips so she could slip his clothes down his strong legs. She lay them across her golden dresser then knelt back on the bed with him. He sat up so she could pull off his blue jacket, which fell away like the daylight sky followed by his shirt's soft white cloud. Then her eyes closed as she fell into the all-consuming space of his arms.

'Son, you cannot go with *her*! She is the selfish slave of the goddess! She basks in her vanity like a cat in its tongue! She is impure!'

They looked back at the screen.

A dream she had had set in ancient Egypt was playing where she was a priestess of Bast who fell in love with a young man from a poor fishing village and took him back to the temple with her. When she first saw him he was leaning against the mud-brick wall of his house playing a small wooden harp. His mother was anxiously warning him to step back inside as the priestess of Bast approached him idly chewing on a lotus stem, her tight black dress clinging to her as she walked like sinuous feline muscles, her golden collar – shining under the hot sun – revealing to whom she belonged.

'Son, do not speak with her.' His mother was a dark shadow in the doorway.

Anger like a black cat's hissing back arched over the girl's mind, making her even more determined to have him. 'I will give him a golden instrument that will never decay beneath his fingers,' she purred.

The scene changed and the priestess was holding up a black stick of burning incense, watching its red head glow as he blew on it. They heard a cat's mating scream in the night, its tongue gleaming red in the torch light, its fangs reflected in the temple columns rising out of the darkness. Their moans of pleasure seemed to flow on the haunted singing. He was not perfect or divine, he would come to an end like all men, but her feeling for him was endless...

Alex gazed at her, glancing back at her Egyptian form in the dream and then down at her present body. He caressed her breasts in the black dress with an exultant sense of expectancy, the rippling silk catching the screen's light. She lay back on the bed so he could push the dress up past her hips and then over her breasts, exposing them. She sat up for an instant again so he could pull it off her completely, and her black hose were cool as shadows shrouding her legs he caressed away with his warm hands. Her panties went next.

'You have gorgeous legs,' he said, and crouching over her licked a straight path up her body with the firm muscle of his tongue all the way from her navel to her heart, then he followed the moist path he had left on her skin, planting light little seed-kisses against her flesh filled with his growing desire. When his tongue at last reached the tip of one of her breasts, she gasped, 'Take me!' spreading her legs for him and reaching down to grip his tight bottom. She hadn't been with a man in a long time, and even then she had never been as fulfilled by anything as she was by the sound of Alex's groan as he thrust his cock into her tight slot. She sensed him hesitate, as if he was afraid of hurting her, but lust got the better of him and he slipped his tongue into her mouth as he jammed his erection all the way into her clinging pussy. She still couldn't believe what was happening and her mental amazement merged with the intense physical pleasure of his penetrations in such a way that she heard herself crying out as if in pain.

'Am I hurting you?' he whispered, gazing steadily down into her eyes even as his hips kept pumping selfishly, energetically between her thighs.

'Oh, no, it just feels so... so good!'

He smiled. 'Can you handle it?'

'Oh, yes, fuck me!' she gasped. 'Fuck me, please!'

He pushed himself up, supporting his weight on his arms so he could watch his big, thick cock rising in and out of her clinging cunt. She clenched her sex around him, stroking and pumping his erection with her vaginal muscles until he groaned and fell on top of her. He rammed his hard-on into her slick pussy with a breathless force that told her how good she felt to him, and that was all she cared about, all she wanted, all she desired, now and forever.

'I'm going to come!' he breathed.

'Oh, yes, come inside me!' she begged.

Reaching beneath her with both hands he clutched the tender cheeks of her ass for even more leverage as he banged her fiercely. Yet the harder he fucked her the more she opened up to him; the more willingly she absorbed and welcomed his violence which felt better than anything. The miraculous cup of her fulfillment literally overflowed when he shot his load inside her, and collapsed into her arms as if the intensity of his climax had wrenched the soul from his body.

# Chapter Six

Elizabeth was in Jim's office waiting for him. It was Monday afternoon. She had always liked his wooden desk and wall-to-wall bookshelves, and the thick, forest-green carpet. He said the decor evoked a forest, the ideas in the books blooming profusely as its leaves and flowers. 'But, unfortunately, not as naturally or beautifully,' he added. 'Most modern philosophers and poets write with the same spirit as a grave digger, trying to make you fall into the cynical hole they're stuck in. Paragraph after paragraph, shovel full after shovel full, with worms for commas.'

'I know,' she agreed, laughing. She remembered this conversation now with her left hand resting on the lily white bud of his computer. Light from the open window fell on her fingers, bare of a golden band – there was no male spirit to whom she belonged as the earth did to the sun. The garden outside was another woman, and holding her in his energetic embrace was Alex. Elizabeth's thoughts had always been strong, flowering vines rising over conventional outlooks, yet it was only the hope of one day experiencing true love's unmitigated warmth that sustained her positive spirit.

Jim had poked his wind-blown brown head into her class that morning as she was talking about Dionysus. 'That's me,' he declared.

The boys laughed, talking all at once trying to catch his attention and create a bigger diversion in their studious day, but he ignored them, staring seriously at Elizabeth. 'Meet me in my office later,' he commanded.

She nodded. The long Sunday stretched behind her with the empty numbness of anesthesia. Nothing had happened except the desperate operation of her mind trying to understand why life worked the way it did, because her emotional survival depended on figuring it out. Alex had left when it was still dark out. 'It's better this way,' he whispered, bending over her, and then he left as swiftly as one of his dream images vanished into the blank screen's impenetrable mist. Yet his reality was an exquisite knowledge all through her body as she closed her eyes to recapture the deep, full sense of him. The memory of his caresses and penetrations filled her inner space with the exciting warmth of stars exploding far away; her limbs sinking into her bed as into primeval sea foam in which everything was deliciously latent. When she woke only a few hours later to a dull gray Sunday she felt completely disoriented. The night flooded back in images that rose and broke violently into each other, beginning with Jim's mischievous arrival at her apartment in the evening, and ending with Alex's deep kiss and departure in the timeless darkness. Then the numbness set in as her mind tried to save her from the suicidal plunge of her heart, yet there was nothing for her to do but pronounce the dreaded diagnosis of Love.

She thought it a painfully significant coincidence that her scheduled lecture Monday morning concerned the polar forces of Apollo and Dionysus, whom she now saw as Alex and Jim.

She heard the door open behind her but didn't turn to look; she was oddly transfixed by the sight of her hand resting in the sunlight. A shadow fell across it and then Jim covered it with his own hand, his breath burning her neck immediately soothed by his cool lips. She didn't move away as he began to caress her, his left hand pressing heavily down on hers so together they looked like two passionately mating spiders. She was as helplessly subject to the desire of these two men as to the laws of physics – with Jim it was Newtonian in that she was bound to fall, but with Alex she had felt the magic curving of time and space in his arms.

'What happened?' Jim turned her to face him, but the answer deflected her eyes away from his to an inner orbit around the memory of Alex's golden head and the irresistible pull of his smiling lips, the horizon into which all her thoughts now sank and from which all her dreams rose.

'I see… the bastard.'

For a breathless moment Jim's anger made her feel happy, but then it only heightened her confused depression. 'You deliberately left us together,' she accused quietly. 'I should hate you. I think I will, when I get the energy. Right now, I just don't care.'

He grasped her hand gently and led her out into the garden adjoining his office. 'You got what you wanted, didn't you?'

His matter-of-fact tone sent a hot, sap-like surge of anger through her. 'It isn't what I wanted.' She freed her hand and walked over to some rose bushes, gratefully losing her thoughts in their rosy whirlpools, seeking to forget herself in their perfectly fulfilled blooms. 'You think I'm too idealistic, don't you, Jim? You don't believe in true love.'

'I just hadn't met the right woman, Elizabeth.'

She gave him a sharp look, but couldn't help admiring the way the faux gold collar of his burgundy shirt glittered around his neck in the sunlight. She was wearing a sleeveless, sky-blue body suit, a necklace of black beads flashing the spectrum whenever she moved, and thin, silver-blue bracelets glimmered cool as Saturn's rings around her wrist when she brushed wind-blown strands of dark hair out of her eyes. 'Aren't you tired of all those bodies?' she demanded, angrily fighting the weakening injection of his stare. 'Don't they all look the same to you by now, like barren plots of land? Wouldn't you like a relationship as strong and beautiful and aspiring to heaven as an oak tree? Surely you must be tired of picking women like flowers just for their looks, and holding them in the vase of your favor for a little while before your interest in them inevitably fades? Don't you want to be able to express all of yourself with one of them?'

He laughed, throwing his head back, and Elizabeth realized this was something he rarely ever did and she was stunned by how beautiful he looked.

He put an arm around her shoulders and they watched the motionless yet dynamic performance of the flowers for a moment in silence. 'You're my blue rose, Elizabeth,' he whispered, 'the magic blue rose of the Arabian Knights. You're the only woman whose opinion of me I care about... whose disfavor hurts me...' He made her face him again. 'Let's go away together and see what happens, or rather, *feel* what happens...'

'Where would we go?' She watched his face approach hers menacingly, but then willingly lost herself in the warm darkness of his kiss.

He drew back. 'Well?'

'Yes!' she sighed.

'Beautiful, we can begin the evening school gets out.' He spoke softly, caressing her hair, and she indulged in the feeling of being a helpless little girl in his arms; her profound innocence trusting him despite how easily she knew he could hurt her. 'I'm taking you to my castle, Elizabeth. I'll stock up on everything we need and together we'll try to find Nirvana. Despite everything they say I'm sure it's very near here.'

A strange wave of relief flooded her, followed by a sinking sense of despair when she realized how glad she was that they weren't actually going far. It was irrational, but it made her feel a little better to know that she would remain near Alex.

# Chapter Seven

Elizabeth didn't see Jim alone again, but every time they encountered each other in the school, he kissed her on the cheek. 'Nirvana in a few days, baby.' He grasped her arm and kissed her mouth, making her realize how much she had missed the firm warmth of his lips against hers. Then at last it was the end of term and grasping her arm in the hallway he whispered into her hair, 'Nirvana tomorrow. I'll pick you up at nine o'clock. Bring everything you'll need for all eternity. I've uprooted my telephone so none of my flowers can reach me. I want to be completely alone with my blue rose, because I have a feeling you're magical, Elizabeth, while all the others will only serve as adornments on my grave.'

\* \* \*

At eight o'clock, when she was finished packing and was thinking about how much she was going to miss her little apartment, especially her Dream Recorder, the phone rang. The hope that it might be Alex still made her heart skip a beat, but only weakly now, impossibly as a butterfly trying to fly through a snow storm — all the days and nights that had already passed since they shared each other's deepest warmth.

The caller was Jim. 'How are you, my beautiful blue one?'

She knelt before the black honeycombs of the display stage and kissed his luminous little form, her red mouth a huge carnivorous flower beside it.

'Now cut that out,' he protested. 'I called to tell you something before I came over. Alex phoned me at the school yesterday. He asked about you, and I told him you were doing very well despite his miserable conduct, for which he wants to apologize to you through me. You see, Elizabeth, he's rather upset with himself, because he's never been unfaithful to his wife before. Are you going to slam the gates of paradise in my face now?'

'No, Jim.' She stood up. At the sound of Alex's name her nerves name had become live wires, and his impotent apology was like water poured over them – it made her rigid with pain and fury. Then she felt lost and hungry as a cat he had given a comforting caress but not taken in, so that she wanted desperately to cry yet also to scratch his selfish face. 'Are you coming to pick me up now?' She crossed her arms, seeking to contain the savage intensity of her emotions, a calmer, higher part of her observing them like a wild animal tamer. His response was to vanish, and she knew he was on his way. 'Thank God! Now I can really forget about Alex.' She was glad, after all, that she was leaving the Dream Recorder behind. 'I can't wait to have his son in my class so I can fail him!'

# Chapter Eight

Lightning struck, blanching the room into the carved relief of a marble tomb and catching the image of their wine glasses raised for a toast like a camera flash.

'We were just photographed,' Jim informed her seriously, the delicate clink of their glasses shattering the night with thunder. His living room could only de described as Draculesque. Beside the cold stone fireplace were two candelabra half as tall as her with sculpted silver hands grasping slender black candles. She felt they could only have been dug up, not from the mere darkness of soil but from that of another dimension were all fantasies are real. 'I was saving these candles for a special night,' Jim went on mildly, following her gaze. 'Will you light them, Elizabeth?'

'Of course.' She took the miniature silver urn he handed her and raised the lid with her thumb.

'The divine spark,' he explained, a smile warming his serious face.

'Where did you get this?' She lit the candles one by one. 'I absolutely love this lighter.' Her slender fingers caressing the urn evoked naked bodies bending over it worshipfully.

'It's yours.'

'But your name is inscribed on the bottom...' She looked into his eyes, the depth of his silence pressing on her heartbeats in the dark room now flickering with candlelight. The black rug was cool and soft against her translucent violet hose (she had long since kicked off her shoes) and silvery curtains shimmering like tears in the corners of her eyes.

He leaned more comfortably back in his chair, stretching his long legs before him and emitting an urgent, sorrowful sound by dipping his finger in the wine and caressing the crystal rim of his glass. 'Aren't you impressed that I even arranged for a thunder storm your first night in my castle, Elizabeth?'

'Not at all, that's child's play for a sorcerer.' She sat down opposite him again in the wingback leather chair.

He smiled but did not look at all amused staring down into his wine.

'Whose blood is it?' she asked lightly. 'One of your flower's, no doubt. You sucked her dry and tossed her away. But I'm too deep for that,' she warned him, 'you'll drown first.'

'I hope so!' he said quietly but fervently.

'Let's play something,' she suggested, because he looked like a boy whose toys had always disappointed him. 'Let's enact something,' she clarified.

'What are you in the mood for?'

She stared at the tiny flames mirrored in his eyes as they opened wide, waiting for her to sow an exciting idea in them.

'I'm thinking...' She wanted to hold on to the wonder of that moment forever, and a vision was imprinted in her mind as lightning flashed again... she saw herself as a naked, living statue, dressed only in the clinging vines of his thoughts and feeling... She shook her head. 'Weird...' she mumbled. 'This wine is getting to me...'

'No, sweet one, it's what I put in it.'

She was stunned. She set her drink down as carefully as an explosive as two consecutive lightning flashes took in the room with a mysteriously discerning glance. 'You put something in our drinks?' she was shocked yet excited, so that her voice came out sounding angrily amused. Jim nodded and she became acutely aware of the beautiful fullness of his hair. 'What?' she demanded.

'Just a touch of something to make the world more magic, no need to concern yourself. So, what shall we change into?'

She wrapped her arms around herself, curling her legs up beneath her as she secretly enjoyed the sensation of seeming to merge with the antique chair she was sitting in. It was beginning to feel infinitely soft and warm, arching over her and enfolding her. She studied her short violet dress with an appreciative wonder, almost tangling her fingers in the black net of her shawl as she adjusted it curiously. 'I don't want to change,' she said contently, glancing up at Jim, and it took her breath away how handsome he looked. Maybe it was the fact that he didn't belong to her that made him seem more sharply beautiful than she was, and she experienced a sudden stab of desire to possess him, to make him all hers.

'I meant that figuratively, silly, lovely one.' He set his wine glass down and leapt out of his chair abruptly. 'Come on, you said you wanted to play something, at least you did before the uncertain petals of your rationally conditioned personality closed over you.'

'Jim!' She laughed in absolute delight and found she couldn't stop, as if she was in a dangerously speeding car and couldn't find the brakes. Then his shadow fell over her and she looked uncertainly up at him, at the soft, dark cloud of hair framing the Lucifer-like beauty and assurance of his face. Her eyes grew wide and empty of all thoughts purely absorbing the vision of him over her. 'I've never met someone like you before,' she whispered.

'Someone like me?' he whispered back.

She breathed, 'Yes!' quickly to mingle her breath with his.

'What would you like to play, baby?' He also seemed to enjoy this invisible grappling of their spirits through their warm breaths.

'You decide, please, Jim. I don't want to think. I'll do anything you say...'

Their lips met and Elizabeth understood why the soul incarnates — their mingled breath was a heaven that inevitably created the desire for bodies in which to grasp each other's wonder. *The soul didn't fall,* she thought angrily, *it dove into a body on purpose!*

Jim moaned and she became fully aware of her hand between his legs rubbing the cool black leather reverently, as if it was the darkness behind everything beginning to take form, the dimensions of time and space erected by the divine column of his desire seeking her worship... She stood up and led him over to a black couch. He spread himself out across it on his back, and in his black shirt and pants he was almost lost to her against the night-deep velvet, making her desperate with desire for him. There was a constant, low rumbling of thunder outside as she quickly unbuttoned his shirt and flung it open. She was drawing him out of the formless universe into a temple of lunar candelabra and curtains like sheets of lightning. The thunder sounded like the engine of a ship, his body floating before her in the night's life-filled, bottomless depths; his pale skin surfacing from the black couch looking almost luminous in its living warmth; his black leather pants slick as snake skins beneath her caressing hands. She unzipped them, and smiled to see that he wasn't wearing any underwear beneath them. She stood up and looked down at him for a moment – at his lean hips designed to rise and fall without effort and expertly navigate waves of pleasure. Then she flung her shawl's black net over his chest and face as she knelt beside him on the couch. He lay with his eyes closed, perfectly motionless, until she buried his cool, soft penis in her mouth, then he moaned and turned his head to one side and then the other as she began sucking him, gently and silently at first then more hungrily and noisily, making lusty slurping sounds with her tongue as she rubbed his stiffening length with her fist, twirling her tongue around his semen-slick head.

'Oh, God, Elizabeth...' His fingers threaded themselves

through her hair. When he came she raised her head slightly and his cum shot up into her mouth like a shower of glimmering stars in the candlelight. He pulled her down into his arms and she lay in them peacefully, raising her hand slightly to watch her shadow caressing him. That she had once lain this way with Alex felt as impossible as the sun rising at midnight. She stared at the shadows from the candle flames flickering overhead, emptying her mind to join their cool yet excited gathering at the high ceiling's table. There was nothing there, yet the rippling darkness felt infinitely rich, as if she could lay it out with her own personal feast of dreams on silver moon platters without end... and then she saw Jim's beautiful flesh-and-blood face floating over her.

# Chapter Nine

'Lets take it slow, baby, terribly, torturously, Tantrically slow. Lets sleep naked together for a week before we make love.' He turned her on her side and pressing her against him caressed her back, gently cradling her soft ass in his hands. 'We can modernize the six month span to six days, our metabolisms run that much faster now.' He made this point with a finger he slipped beneath the elastic of her panty – her pussy was moist and ready for him.

'Oh, Jim...'

'I'm serious.' He passed his hand soothingly down her thighs.

'All right, but let's make it truly contemporary Tantra and shorten the span to six minutes, please.'

'In the past, lovers gave each other locks of hair because their bodies were more inaccessible to each other, for one reason or another. Now it's souls that can't be had while bodies come a dime a dozen,' he lectured quietly. 'First our desires should have a long, silent conversation, and write a poem of our emotions, so that after we burn out the flesh's brief page our hearts can rise together like the magical wings of the Phoenix from its ashes...' He sighed. 'But you know all that, my sweet, ancient history teacher.' He pulled her up into a sitting position. 'And you're mine.' He whipped off her dress and pushed her back down to look at her. 'You're shaped like a classical statue,' he observed in his most formal principle's voice. 'A slenderized version, of course, with small but exquisitely round and perfect breasts, and a completely wondrous, tight waist flowing into deliciously tender hips. And your little belly makes a perfect love cushion, just enough soft flesh for me to rise and fall against comfortably.'

Elizabeth flung her arms back and clung to the edge of the couch so as to resist pulling him down on top of her. 'Jim, please...'

'Yes, sweet, one?' He cocked his head innocently to one side.

She closed her eyes, breathing deeply and slowly bending her legs, the soft velvet beneath her thighs almost too delicious for her to bear. 'Stop it, Jim, please, take me...'

'Just remember, Elizabeth, that the normal rule of life is that when you don't have something, you want it, but when you have it, you don't want it that much anymore, and that this is precisely the mortal law we are seeking to transcend with this experiment.'

She opened her eyes again and stared intently into his. 'Perhaps death is the only exception to this law: you don't have it and you don't want it, but when you finally get it, you find that you do.'

He considered this. 'That would be a nice consolation prize for all our anxiety, wouldn't it?'

'Yes... kiss me.'

'No.'

'Please...'

'No...' He rode the word from her eyes down to her navel so that she seemed to feel the final note sink into it, and this somehow calmed her.

'You're not serious about this Tantra business, are you?'

'What's the matter?' he sounded surprised as he lay back down beside her, propping himself on an elbow to keep the undulating landscape of her body in view. 'You should want to put some ancient techniques into practice to see if they really work.'

'I've never liked Buddhism and the whole business of spending your life desiring not to desire anything,' she said fervently.

'But don't you want to help me come in my brain instead of in you?' he whined like a child denied a special treat, yet she sensed that deep down he actually wanted to believe different, elevating forms of experience were possible with her.

'Do you really want to?' she asked seriously.

'Yes. Although... wait a minute... didn't I walk into your class once when you were discussing the ancient Egyptian method of mummification?'

'Yes, but what has that got to do with Tantric sex?'

'And weren't you describing how they liquefied the brain to pull it out through the nostrils and then threw it away?'

'Yes.'

'Then why the hell should I come in my brain if it's such a disposable commodity?'

'I don't know.' She laughed.

'The Egyptians valued the heart above all else, they considered it the seat of understanding, the home of the soul, and the brain only its secretary, right?'

'So to speak.' She was listening to him, but her eyes kept gliding the soft wings of their gaze over him.

'Then I would like to come in my heart. Didn't they give it a nice little urn with a jackal's head? Pay attention to me, Elizabeth, I'm serious about all this.'

'About what?'

'About where I want to come.'

'Oh, God, Jim.'

'I'm serious,' he insisted.

'Yes, but you're creating an unsavory metaphysical pizza combining these two religions.'

He laughed more joyously than she had ever heard him laugh before, but then he appeared even more serious. 'What do you suppose those Tantric Buddhists experienced when they channeled their orgasm up into their mind? Wasn't it supposed to be like dying, an out of body blissfulness, a sense of wholeness with everything, a divine feeling of power, the beautiful brown body of the girl like the earth beneath you, completely at your service?'

'Yes, except that she was sitting on top of him.'

'Really?'

'Yes, and probably frowning because she didn't get to come, much less channel anything into her mind. She was only an instrument he was never allowed to see again. She stood for the pure metaphysical force of woman, so it wouldn't do for the initiate to become fond of her individual, incarnate personality. This would only bond him even more strongly to the earthly plain, and her role was to help him transcend it.'

'Wow.'

'Yes, I'm sure you can relate, but I've always hated the belief that man fell when he incarnated in a body and that life is nothing but a complicated, careful struggle to ascend again,

in which woman naturally stands for the matter binding man's once blissfully free spirit, which ultimately makes him look like a damned klutz. I mean, what happened when he was floating

formless in heaven? He accidentally tripped and fell, over God knows what, and woman caught him graciously but greedily in the arms of manifestation, and always tries to keep him from ascending to his divine bachelor's club in the sky? I mean, Jesus Christ!'

'Well then, what *did* happen, beautifully angry one?'

'Man is the universe's unfathomable force and woman is his star. Her body is the world fashioned by his desire... that's the nature of her soul, his eternal experience. Even Tantrism recognized the highest state of being as Shiva united with his Shakti.'

'Elizabeth, will you marry me?'

She stretched languidly, the tone of his voice flowing warmly through her. 'You'll get tired of living with a blue rose, Jim. You'll miss your wild flowers, and dizzy daisies, and titillating tulips...'

'Elizabeth...'

'Your cute carnations, and your playful pussy willows...'

'Elizabeth!'

'Yes, Jim?' She smiled, trying to remember more flowers.

'Are you finished?'

'No, there are voluptuous violets, and crazy chrysanthemums, and-'

'And you can have them all for your bridal bouquet. I'm witheringly tired of variety.'

'Would you invite them all to our wedding?'

'No, I'd start with Alex and his wife.'

She bit her lip, desperately holding back tears as everything she had felt in the last few weeks flooded back and painfully broke the comforting dam this night with Jim had begun to erect.

'Oh, baby, I'm sorry!' She had never heard him sound so sincere, almost frightened. 'I'm sorry!' he breathed, wrapping her in his arms.

'It's not your fault.' She caressed him, kissing his neck, and the sense of him grasping and lifting her hips was unexpectedly followed by swift explosions of joy in which she vaguely heard her own cries. He raised himself to witness his violent stabs, and she truly saw him then – an exquisitely selfish killer whose understanding penetration of her inner life was, ultimately, for his own stimulation and pleasure.

# Chapter Ten

Jim and Elizabeth were sitting outside on his porch having breakfast at three o'clock in the afternoon. It had rained all night, so there were a few sun-dried worms scattered over the wooden boards, and she was thinking how, one day, his sex would be forever soft in them.

'Being intense doesn't help you in the end, does it?' she wondered out loud.

Jim's eyes on her were darker than ever, but he was smiling softly, as if his lips blew up naturally that way under the pleasant breeze. 'There's really no difference between the living and the dead,' he said, 'except that they're completely naked.'

She smiled and finished her second orange juice.

'Look at it this way, blue one.' Jim's voice penetrated her musings. 'Heaven's purity is like clean white sheets filled with the all surrounding warmth of your lover.'

'Oh, I like that.' She studied him across the glass table where he sat in a white wicker chair in his skimpy black swimsuit. They were planning to spend the afternoon in his pool. The porch was shaped like a pyramid and they were at its apex surrounded by large old trees acting as the living sentinels of their privacy. 'But what reality do analogies have, Jim?'

'Reality *is* analogies, or images, don't you see? They're energy's awareness; they're the nature of its consciousness. What

*Moonlit Dreams*

we experience as beauty is unbound power shaping itself...'

'Like an artist expresses himself in his work.'

'Exactly, my sweet, sweet one.'

'But perhaps it would be better stated as unbound love...'

'Perhaps, but we suffer when we become too attached to the perishable form.'

'Yes, I know,' she said impatiently, 'but I can't help being terribly fond of you as you are now.'

'That's all right. I'll always be me, just a little more intense each time I take form.'

She stared down at her violet swimsuit, very pleased with this statement. 'How often do you drink mysteriously enhanced wine like we had last night? That was unbelievably intense.'

He contemplated the toast he hadn't touched. 'Only on special occasions.'

'Why do I get the feeling that these occasions are not infrequent enough to make them truly special?'

'Because you don't trust me, my blue one.'

'Why should I, pray tell?'

'Don't forget that I asked you to marry me, Elizabeth, and that I meant it.'

'Right!' She looked down shyly.

'You seemed to enjoy yourself.'

'I had no choice.'

'Perhaps that's what you enjoyed the most.'

'Perhaps...' She was delightfully overwhelmed by sadomasochistic possibilities that made the sunlight feel even hotter on her bare arms and legs.

'I'd be happy to help you explore them all.' He seemed to read her mind, and she found herself remembering a day in elementary school when she pressed her desk hard against her stomach, hoping that no one would notice, because she was irresistibly excited listening to her teacher talk about Mayan sacrifices.

'Are you finished eating?'

His sharply impatient tone made desire instantly burn through her like venom, his smile slipping between her heart beats on the beautiful serpent of his lips.

He stood up, grasped her hand, and led her to the center of his sunlit lawn. He peeled off her swimsuit and then lay face down on the grass beneath her. He didn't need to tell her what he wanted her to do. She crouched over his face, kissing his mouth with the lips of her labia as she rested her warm cheek on his cool black swim trunks. She gasped as his tongue roamed like a curious little animal inside her pussy, and then moaned with a deep appreciation of its adventurous energy. The trees seemed to be swimming in the bright heat. 'Oh, Jim, please...'

'All right,' he sighed.

Pushing herself to her feet, she eagerly peeled off his sticky shorts. His cock sprung out of them so hard and long the swift way she straddled him and plunged his erection inside her felt like suicide. She cried out as the sun beat relentlessly down on them, her greedy motion excavating jewels of sweat from his gleaming flesh. She showered her hair over his face, its brown strands a golden curtain in the light.

'You're so beautiful, Elizabeth!' He ran his fingers through her hair. 'You're so fucking beautiful!'

His fierce praise struck joyous chords inside of her, ecstasy's melody overflowing her veins dissolving her in the wet heat of his arms.

# Chapter Eleven

The terrible shock of her parents' death in a car crash when she was twenty-two, and a growing disillusionment with her actual experiences as contrasted to her ideal expectations, caused Elizabeth to become unusually gregarious for her nature, shedding her natural shyness in a need for experiences to distract her from her sadness. Her senses reared their heads like fiery dragons and demanded an endless supply of fresh male meat. Her grief, and the abrupt confrontation with death, made her body desperately hungry, yet the more blindly she fed it, the more it blocked her re-entry into the realm of profound sensibility in which she had always lived. Her intoxicated sexuality was like a wild black cat with a terrible grip on her heart's inspirational flights, her sorrow at her parents' death curdling into anger at life's limitations. The discrepancy between her imagination and what the mortal plain could actually offer played a big part in the unhinging of her self control. Instead of the exciting freedom she had always idealistically looked forward to – the power to experience all she had dreamed about – adulthood only brought with it more restrictions. Boring responsibilities loomed ahead that made school look like fun, and her dream man was nowhere to be seen. With dimensions closing painfully in on her, dating a different man every week seemed to provide magical keys leading out of the mundane into a more enchanted space ruled by her desire.

It took over two years for Elizabeth to realize that all sleeping around did was help her turn off her mind and all its anxieties about the future. On her twenty-fifth birthday, she finally sobered up into a creative depression. She began to express her magical view of life and love in drawings, cast off meaningless sex, and turned to chastity, because the one hope she still cherished was finding a man with a soul to match the passionate depth of her own. She went back to school and got her Master's in education as she supported herself hopping from one clerical job to another. Her degree was still warm when she answered Jim's intriguing ad for an ancient history teacher and, after a five-hour interview, she was awarded both the job and his stimulating friendship. It seemed to Elizabeth that they talked about absolutely everything that first day. He explained how bored he had become with the routine of being a rock star, forced to tour for six months then to grind out another album whether the band was inspired or not. 'I hated the repetition of the same songs on stage, the repetition of cities all the same, and the fact that I knew most of my audience wasn't listening to my lyrics and trying to make their life better, more meaningful. What I said was usually a compromise anyway, because I could never put my real poetry into a popular song. After I'd made a million, and slept with just about as many women, at sound check the empty concert halls started looking to me like God's mouth yawning. I knew I had to get out before the world rolled over away from me and I lost all my energy to be truly inspired.' After talking to him, Elizabeth had found the strength to put into practice the fact that creativity was the only cure for her profound boredom.

Now at the "castle" days and nights flowed by with the timeless rhythm of his penetrations, the shore of hours blissfully diffused by waves of pleasure. She was showering alone one evening, the sunset a burning jewel set in the small circular window of the water-blue bath tub. White lights flickered across the cool coral walls in imitation of the sun shining on waves overhead, all her cares and concerns dissolving like human legs into the joyful energy of a mermaid's tail as she lathered herself up and washed her hair. Jim was down in his cellar selecting a wine for dinner, after which he always enjoyed teasing and flustering his cook, a petite, middle-aged French woman. He followed her around the kitchen as she worked, stalking her mouse-like reserve like a cat with his sharp sensual humor.

She walked out of the misty bathroom wrapped in a white towel feeling peaceful as a cloud dreamily drifting through erotic memories into the bedroom where she kept her things. She sat on the edge of the bed and let the towel slip off her to the floor as she wondered what to wear. Her long wet hair coiled in thin serpents over her white breasts, her mirror image across from her looking like a Cretan girl, her pet house snakes hungry for milk.

'Who shall I be tonight?' she asked her reflection, watching her naked body walk with haunting gravity to the end of the bed, twirling around to hug the post of the old-fashioned canopy. She rubbed her breasts and belly slowly against the hard wood, its carved edges exciting her. She wanted him to tie her up again, like the night they played Dracula's Castle...

Jim wore an elegant black cape and bought her a classic white nightgown for the occasion. 'Run outside,' he instructed. 'I'll count to one-hundred. Then, my dear, I'll come after you, and you'd better pray I don't catch you.' He laughed wickedly, throwing back his head.

She clapped happily at his performance, but the expression in his eyes sent her flying out the door. She ran past the pool, almost supernaturally still and luminous in the moonlight, and then through a side yard. She cried out when a branch seemed to reach out and grasp her gown's flying ghost, and the leaves whispered sinisterly, 'This is where you belong... come lie here beneath us...' making her run even faster. She collided with Jim in his black cape so abruptly that she screamed.

'It's no use,' he whispered. 'Don't fight it, baby. It won't hurt very much, if you're good...' He lifted her in his arms, and she lay her head trustingly on his shoulder. He set her down beneath a tree, and she cried out again when he ripped her brand new nightgown down the front and wrenched it off her. 'Don't be frightened, sweet one, just do as I say.' His whisper seemed to be a part of the breeze sighing through branching veins. 'Lean back against the trunk, lovely one.'

She obeyed, hypnotized by his tone, and she watched in growing excitement and trepidation as he wrapped the remains of her dress around her wrists, then lifted her arms and tied the cloth to an upper branch. 'Oh, God,' she moaned. 'Jim?'

He stepped back to look at her. The bark was hard and rough against her bare skin, and leaves tickled her raised arms with a timeless calm, cooling teasing her pulsing sense of vulnerability. He approached her, his cape an expanding black cloud swallowing her moonlit body as he took her in his arms...

'Hurry up, Elizabeth, we have an unexpected guest!'

She was shocked out of the memory's depth by Jim's voice yelling up the stairs, and felt debilitated for a moment by an emotional case of the bends. 'A guest?' She unwillingly dressed.

# Chapter Twelve

She chose a sleeveless dark-green dress that fell to mid-thigh, wide black silver-studded bracelets (which she saw as the star filled expanses of night sky over the passionate jungle of her figure) and silver earrings that evoked moonlit pyramids within her dark hair. Her eyes were murderously intent as she prepared herself, wondering who this unexpected guest might be and all the time certain it was one of his women. This outfit was a figurative way to grow claws with which to swiftly, smilingly, scratch the girl's eyes out with horrified envy as she, Elizabeth, strolled into the room with the confidence of a wild cat.

Walking down the main staircase, she fixed her gaze on the round emerald ring Jim had given her, caressing it like a miniature crystal ball. *He's mine*, she thought. *I'll kill them all if I have to because he's mine!* She heard his soft voice inside the plant-filled room where they had breakfast on rainy mornings, and paused for a moment in the large entrance hall. The floor was made of smooth, multi-colored pebbles designed to give his guests the impression of having landed on some exotic shore, and lamps that looked like distant light houses were evenly distributed across sea-blue walls painted like cresting waves. Bracing herself, she stepped into the small room with the swift intent of a cat raiding a bird cage, expecting to see the delicately pretty blonde who had visited him at the school recently. She saw a living flash of gold in the shadows, and then the room seemed to spin around her. Plants, lamps and tables for a moment all orbited Alex's body standing as forcefully still as the eye of a storm before her.

'Elizabeth's been staying with me since school got out,' Jim was saying. 'We've been trying to achieve Nirvana. We haven't yet, but trying is so much fun, who the hell cares.'

'Hello, Elizabeth.' Alex's tone was cool and smooth as the neck of one of his guitars.

Her body instantly felt taut and vulnerable to the pressure of his thoughts. 'Hello, Alex.'

He was wearing a soft black leather jacket and scarf, the hands that had caressed her politely concealed in the pockets of his black pants.

She closed the door behind her and approached Jim, finding a soothing gravity in his half open light-blue cotton shirt and soft brown hair. Alex's light-ray-straight golden strands almost blinded her, his body in black leather shattering her thought-veined awareness like the void of space.

'Will you stay for dinner, seeing as it's almost ready,' Jim asked, not looking at her.

Alex smiled. 'No, I can't, thanks.'

'But we insist.' Jim smiled back.

'No we don't,' she said quietly, lost between Alex's cool blue eyes like distant planets she knew could never sustain her life, and the desperate need for Jim to support her with his gaze.

'That's not polite, Elizabeth.' He only glanced at her. 'One should always insist. So try and convince him to stay, like a good hostess, while I inform Louise.'

Incredulously, she watched the blue atmosphere of his shirt and the brown world of his head leave the room.

Alex stood impossibly before her like the coldness of space, so that she felt herself floating in a terrible void bereft of any possible direction. She looked away from him, almost collapsing onto the couch behind her. She curled her legs up beneath her and stared at him with the territorial stillness of a cat as he seated himself in a chair across from her.

'So, how've you been?' she inquired languidly.

'Good,' he answered softly. 'How have you been, Elizabeth?'

'I've never been happier,' she replied sincerely. 'It sounds trite, but it's true.'

'I'm glad.' He smiled and she knew all through her body that he meant it. His expression slowed her blood to a honey-like richness she could almost feel. Then she wasn't so sure what she had said was true, and bit her lip. 'Jim has an incredible place here,' he commented.

'Yes.' Unwillingly, she remembered the way Alex had playfully looked down at her, whispering, 'Ten, nine, eight, seven, six, five, four, three, two...' while he dipped his cock into her gently, and then he said firmly, 'One!' as he thrust into her hard and deep. 'Again?' he asked, smiling when she opened her eyes. She nodded and they played this little game for a while, counting faster every time, until he couldn't stop thrusting...

Her lips parted as she sought to catch her breath remembering. She looked away from him, and it helped a little.

'What is it?' he asked gently.

'What is it?' she repeated, glancing back at him. 'Nothing... it's just nice to see you again.'

'I know...'

Jim returned. 'Well, has she convinced you yet?'

'No, I still can't stay, but I'll take a rain check.' Alex rose. 'Thanks for your advice. I hope it works. I'm starting to get worried.'

'What's wrong?' Elizabeth went and stood beside Jim.

'His son's been having nightmares and is afraid of going to sleep,' he explained, finally looking fully at her, and she had to resist the urge to fall on her hands and knees and rub herself against his legs she experienced such a pure, safe sense of devotion to him. 'So I told him what I used to do as a kid. I'd turn my head on the pillow and each position was a different channel. I had a dinosaur channel, a mystery channel, and so on, and depending on what I wanted to dream

about I'd turn my head to the right or to the left or lay facing straight up. It usually worked, too. I dreamed with whatever I wanted to dream about.'

'I'll try to get Mark to do that.' Alex preceded them into the hall. 'I'll tell him that he has the power to control what he dreams about, that all he has to do is avoid the nightmare channel. He might stop being afraid of going to sleep if he thinks he can avoid the bad dreams.'

'And if he thinks he can, he probably will.' Elizabeth encouraged him.

'Let's hope so.' Jim entwined his fingers in hers like an octopus as they stood surrounded by the cresting blue waves of his walls.

Alex left and she looked up at him, and she knew her smile was as enigmatic to him as the crescent moon by the subtle frown creasing his brow. They stared at each other, and she felt they were both resisting the desire to say, 'I love you' because it would make Alex's visit a cliché in a story with an expectedly trite end. 'Shall we go eat?' he asked, and her smile deepened as her eyes closed. Since the first evening in her apartment, he sometimes said this before he began kissing her hungrily. This time he didn't, so she looked at him again.

'Jim, did you really mean it when you asked me to marry you?'

His eyes gripped her pulse. 'No.' Her heart stopped. 'But I do now.' He smiled.

'Jim, do you really?'

He sighed. 'Oh, God, do I have to get on my knees?' He lifted her in his arms suddenly and carried her up the stairs looking into her eyes the whole time, so that she felt it was her devotion to him that was taking them higher and higher. He kicked the balcony door open onto the soft atmosphere of evening. There was a sorrowful red stain on the western horizon, the garden below already covered by a mournful veil of darkness woven by tree limbs as they rustled whispered prayers.

He sat her on the balcony railing and she clung to him, her arms a vice around his neck, her legs gripping his slender body. 'Let go,' he whispered.

'But I'll fall!'

'Don't you trust me?' His voice was dangerously soft, hypnotically concentrated with all the mysterious force of his willpower. 'How can you marry someone you don't trust with your life, Elizabeth? I know you're afraid of heights... no, don't look back, look at me, look into my eyes and trust me...'

'Jim...'

'If you love me, then you can't be afraid of anything with me. You're afraid of heights, that's a weakness, but if you transfer that fear into trust for me, you'll lose it and become stronger.'

'No, I won't! I trust you not to let go of me, but that doesn't eliminate my fear of falling.'

'But it should, don't you see, Elizabeth? The reason you were afraid of heights is because you didn't know anyone who could hold all of you, but now I'm here, so you needn't be afraid anymore, of anything. You can't burn, you can't drown, you can't fall, you can't be hurt by anything, only I can hurt you, because we love each other, and that's what burns in fire, what rises and falls in heights, what closes in to embrace, what surrounds and lifts you like water. It's the whole world, so how can you be afraid of anything now?'

'Oh, Jim...' His tone was drugging her; her hold was weakening. 'I worship you, but I'm still terrified of falling...'

'Then you don't really believe in love's divine nature, if you did, you'd know that mine will hold you up...'

'Oh, Jim...' Her arms slipped from around his neck. She caressed his chest, clinging to the open folds of his shirt and more securely to his belt, looking up into his eyes. It completely hit her then what a miracle he was, a pure joy rushing up her spine wiping out her mind for a moment, his intense stare like a socket connecting her pulse with the energy in everything. She raised her arms like a ballerina and arched back into the void, conscious only of his hard warmth around her waist.

'Elizabeth!' He pulled her back up violently.

She clung to him, her head spinning with blood, and with the much more dizzying realization that she had beaten him at his own game.

# Chapter Thirteen

They appeared in the dining room hand in hand, but each one lost in his own thoughts. Jim gallantly pulled out her chair, its dark wooden back carved in the shape of the moon seed flower, the velvet green cushion a cool patch of moss.

'Thank you, my lord.' She smiled, seating herself at the polished oak table whose surface she had stared at in awe the night he laced their wine, mesmerized by its golden spirals framed by a darker grain. 'Oh, Jim, aren't these beautiful?' She had exclaimed, bending over the gloaming surface, caressing it and resting her cheek against its cool, perfect smoothness. It fascinated her that there was no organic roughness to it; flowing clean and bright as energy beneath her hand.

Jim examined the table with the same wide-eyed wonder. 'Pretty awesome,' he agreed, and pulled her into the kitchen, switching on the overhead light. By then, the entire house was lit up, because they had wandered into all the rooms and studied everything in this way. He opened the refrigerator and she leaned against him, one hand on his shoulder, one on the buckle of his belt. He gently picked up an egg, staring at it as if he had never seen one in his life.

'Look how smooth it is,' she said softly, as if a loud voice would disturb its subtle gravity.

'It's perfect!' he yelled.

She winced.

'They're all different yet all the same, so smooth and fragile yet so strong.' he observed. 'And each one has a little golden sun inside it swimming in the milky, galactic substance from which worlds are made and life is fashioned... it's a little spirit-sun shaping its own body...'

'Isn't it wondrous?'

'Yes.' He flung it against a wall.

Elizabeth stared at the orange mess for a moment, and then burst out laughing. 'That wasn't very nice of you, Jim!'

'Why aren't you sad?' He glared at her. 'You're supposed to whine and tell me about all the trouble it went to to get this far, and that now it won't even have the honor of being consumed by another living thing. It's totally wasted now, thanks to me. You were supposed to be upset, Elizabeth. Where's your compassion?'

'But it didn't go to any trouble, silly. It had a good time becoming itself, and I'm sure being smashed gave it a real rush.'

'You witch,' he murmured, and shoved her towards the egg-stained wall. 'Go and lick it up and apologize for your lack of reverence to its poor, shattered life.'

'Fuck you! Go lick it up yourself. You're the one who killed it!'

To her amazement, he strolled over to the wall, his tight, royal-blue shirt beautifully brilliant against the bright mess, his body a master painting in front of a dirty palette.

'Oh, no Jim, don't!' She ran over to him.

She was too late; he was already licking the wall, and the sight of his tongue – a muscle embodying his invisible force gleaming in the bright light threw her into a frenzy. She grabbed his shoulders and pulled his egg-stained tongue into her mouth. 'Yuck!' She shoved him away again.

'You'll pay for that,' he warned her in his gentlest, most potentially dangerous tone.

She laughed and ran out of the kitchen.

He caught her at the dining room table and bent her face-down over it. 'Let's see how good it looks to you now…'

Louise served Jim's soup cautiously, as if it had come from the crater of a volcano which, like his tumultuous personality, was only temporarily dormant.

'Elizabeth and I are getting married,' he announced, and she nearly dropped the ladle.

'He's not joking either, Louise… at least I don't think so.'

'Is it true?' The older woman frowned as she gently dished out Elizabeth's serving, the size of which she had learned to increase after the first night, when it became clear that Jim's new flame could eat just as much, or more, than he could, and thoroughly resented being given less.

Jim sighed, pouting, and stirred his soup lackadaisically. 'No one ever believes me.'

'I do, sweet baby, because if you didn't really want to marry me you wouldn't nearly have thrown me off the balcony.'

'That's true.'

Louise froze. 'You almost did *what*?'

'You can't marry someone you don't trust with your life, Louise,' he explained amiably. 'So I sat her on the balcony railing and told her to let go, that's all.'

'You're a monster!' she declared, and disappeared into the kitchen with her usual air of having fed the lions and getting out as quickly as possible.

That evening, however, Elizabeth and Jim didn't laugh. They stared at each other, and after a moment she set her spoon down, lowering her eyes. 'I'm not hungry…'

'Let's go.' He grabbed the wine bottle and pulled her up with the forcefulness that was making her feel more feminine and more beautiful by the day. The strength of his character both completely relaxed and challenged her, so that it was absolutely no effort at all to express herself. He led her out to the pool, setting the bottle down and stripping all his clothes

*Moonlit Dreams*

off in the time it took her to remove her boots. 'No, wait,' he commanded as she was about to pull off her dress. 'You look like the jungle tonight... let's play Hunter... Run!"

\* \* \*

'Jim, lets go inside, I'm getting cold.' They were in the pool. She was back against the wall, floating with her legs around him as they shared the wine bottle. He kept it on the ledge behind her, holding it up to her lips whenever he decided it was time again. She was deliciously trapped.

'Another little sip for my baby?'

'Aren't you cold?'

'Elizabeth, you have a lot to learn, sweet one. You've heard that love conquers all? Well, it begins with the weather, the basic, elementary forces of nature.' He penetrated her swiftly and suddenly as an attacking shark, moving away from the wall so she could rise and fall around his erection to her heart's content in the water's sensual lack of gravity. 'Are you cold now, baby?'

'Oh, no...'

'This is what it's like on the moon,' he said, and her pussy eagerly clung to his cock in response to his deep, story-teller's voice. 'Silvery liquid air where lovers are always one, because there's no gravity that makes them heavy and hard...'

'But I like it when you're hard.' She bit his neck, moaning as he gripped her hips and controlled the rhythm of her pussy sliding up and down his hard-on.

'There... I want to tell you a story and you can't come until I'm finished. Ready?'

'Oh, yes...'

'It's about a golden snake and a black pussy cat.'

'Oh, Jim, yes...?'

'One day, the golden snake was cruising along the road, being his usual introverted and extroverted self. He was on his way to the setting sun, because he had noticed that its rays coiled into a ball, just like him, every evening. He thought perhaps it was his own reflection, and wanted to merge with it to see what would happen. Along the way, he enjoyed squeezing pretty little creatures to death, because they were warm and he was cold, and the way they shuddered as they gave their young lives to him made him feel less old and alone…'

She felt him abruptly sucked into the whirlpool of an orgasm. 'No, I want to hear the rest,' she pleaded, burying his erection deep inside her and not moving.

I'm sorry, sweet one, where was I? Oh, yes, old and alone…'
She kissed his neck tenderly.

'Then, one day, a black pussy cat crossed his path. He caught her, and as he wrapped himself around her, she began to purr. This was strangely pleasing and soothing to him, but as he squeezed tighter with pleasure her purring stopped. The curious disappointment he experienced weakened his murderous grip and, to his delight, she began purring again. So the golden snake asked the black pussy cat if she was the darkness into which he saw his reflection descend every night. She meowed that she was, and to this day, they still journey together toward the mysterious merging in the West.'

She wanted to tell him that she loved the story, but could only moan everything felt so beautiful.

'You can come now, baby,' he urged.
'Oh, Jim…'
'All right… yes, baby…'
'Oh, God…'
'You've got him trapped between your legs, that's why it hurts. Let go and He'll take you with him, I promise…'

# Chapter Fourteen

They were lying on Jim's bed, soft, white and large as a cloud. They were devouring a bag of crackers, and a circle of yellow cheese that had lain like the sun between them, but now it was almost gone. He shoved another gold-laden brown cracker into her mouth, and she kicked her legs in protest, unable to yell at him until she swallowed.

'Stop it, I'm full, Jim.'

'Nonsense, you're never full, you're a greedy little witch, you're insatiable. Have another one.'

'No!' she rolled off the bed, watching three other Elizabeth's do the same in wall-to-wall mirrors. She glanced up to see her lovely smiling face looking down, and up, at herself. She always got the impression that was her truest self – her soul descending into its own experience and looking up at its own power. 'Jim…' She was going to tell him that his room was disgustingly sleazy, but then realized this was a conditioned reaction, and that what she really felt was a sort of awe, as if they were in the temple of some unknown pagan form of worship.

'Yes, exquisite one?' he began removing the remains of their meal from the bed, and she watched his three figures in motion.

'I feel like I'm in a temple.'

'You are, and guess who's the sacrificial victim? Come here.' He lay back comfortably against some pillows as she walked around the foot of the bed and stood beside him. The room was lit by a dim silvery light coming from a lamp resembling the full moon suspended in the center of the room, so that his naked flesh emerged in supple, gentle waves from the shadows.

'You know what I used to play when I was about eleven or twelve?' She addressed his toes as if their small round heads were her audience, and they wiggled excitedly for her to go on. 'I used to play Mayan sacrifice. I was the victim being carried up to the altar and spread across the cold, hard stone. The knife was my mother's letter opener, coming down over my heart slowly. It excited me the way my breasts rose and fell with my terrified gasps... The idea of an intense man cutting out my heart for magical purposes really turned me on.' She stopped as it occurred to her that she shouldn't tell Jim Grant that, because anybody else would have thought it exotically strange, but he would take it seriously. Then she realized this was precisely why she had told him.

'Elizabeth, dear, that would be a bit messy. What would my cleaning lady say?' With lightning speed he gripped her wrists and pulled her onto the bed, rolling on top of her and pinning her arms above her head. 'What else did you play when you were thirteen, witch?'

When he used that tone, she became weak with pleasure.

'Tell me, witch!' He stared into her eyes and her legs parted helplessly. 'You'll let me cut your heart out because you know a witch never dies, she just lies in the dark ground,' he kissed her until she couldn't breath, 'and even the worms fall under her spell and make love to her, like this.' He let go of one of her wrists and slid two fingers inside her, wriggling them around. Her back arched with the sudden pleasure, and with her free hand she rubbed his palm against her vulva. 'Mm...'

'Mm,' he mocked. 'See, you're insatiable. How many times have I taken you today already?'

'It's only because I love you.' She gripped the back of his neck passionately.

'Like you love Alex?'

Suddenly, the sensation between her legs felt like pain. 'I love *you*,' she insisted.

'You love me?' He kept prodding her pussy with his fingers and her soul with his hard stare.

'Yes, and you know it!'

'I do?'

'Yes…' She started to cry, turning her head from side to side in weak, desperate denial of his accusations.

He slipped his fingers out of her tight, resisting sex and flung her leg over one of his shoulders. 'What did he do to you?' He thrust the words into her.

'Oh, God, Jim!' Tears ran down her face as she tried to look into his eyes, but he was watching himself rising and falling against her as if he thoroughly resented this trap he was caught in. The harder he tried to beat her away, the more she twined tendrils of pleasure through his veins. She lay limp beneath him, her eyes and cheeks burning with tears, her body with the pleasure of his penetrations turned to acid by his mood. 'Jim!'

'Shut up. I'm sure you let him do anything he wanted to you, didn't you?'

'Oh, God…'

'Didn't you?'

'Oh, God, please stop!'

'You still want him, don't you? If he ever called you and asked you to meet him somewhere, you would, wouldn't you? Wouldn't you, bitch?'

'Yes! Yes, I would, you bastard! Let go of me! I hate you! I hate you… Oh, God… I love you…' He had slowed his relentless driving rhythm and was kissing her cheeks, curiously licking her tears, as if he had made her cry just so he could enjoy doing this.

'It's okay.' He smiled down at her. 'You wanted me to cut your heart out, didn't you?'

'Oh, God, I love you, Jim!'

'I know, baby. If you didn't, you would have lied to me.'

'But I *don't* want him,' she lied now desperately.

'Yes you do,' he chided her gently, kissing her again and caressing her cheek with his. 'Just like I wouldn't mind getting blown away by Nancy or going down on Julie, she's so sweet.'

'You don't love me,' she gasped as if her soul were deflating. She closed her eyes.

'You're heart is finally in my hands, isn't it, Elizabeth?' he said in his normal, soft voice.

She didn't move; she couldn't. The will that made her muscles work had hopelessly dissolved. She took the rhythm of his body the way a rock accepts a stream's relentless current.

'Elizabeth,' he whispered. 'Elizabeth…' He pulled his cock out of her and teased her slick, warm opening with his cool head. 'Sweet one, I need you to look into my eyes so I can give you your heart back.' He slid his erection inside her again, lowering her leg gently and resting comfortably on top of her. 'Open yours eyes,' he said firmly.

She obeyed like a dead person listening to a voice coming from high above through a deep weight of darkness. Then she saw him looking at her the way he had in the hall that afternoon as he carried her up the stairs; as he held her on the balcony; as he pulled her up from the table; as he fucked her on the grass when they were playing Hunter; as he held the wine bottle up to her lips in the pool; the way he had looked at her after telling her about the golden snake and the black pussy cat. 'Jim, all I know is that nothing means anything without you, that-'

'Sush, baby, you don't have to write a term paper on it. We're engaged.'

# Chapter Fifteen

Elizabeth was back in her apartment. She held it fondly against her heart for a moment, as if listening to a seashell. Living had become so tumultuous, so deep and exciting with Jim, she felt months had come and gone like giant waves since she last saw her home, but it had actually only been a few weeks.

Leaning against the front door, he observed her meditative stance in the middle of the living room. 'Would you like to keep it?' He slipped his hands into his pockets, and she felt he had just placed her apartment casually into them. 'I'll pay the rent on it so you can have your own little hideaway.'

'I can keep it?' She didn't know why, but it struck her as a dangerous idea.

'Yes, Elizabeth, you can have anything you want now, so you'd better get used to it.'

'Oh, Jim!' She ran and hugged him.

'Okay, collect whatever you want to bring with you while I call my answering service. Everyone probably thinks I've died.'

'Oh, no.' She grasped his shoulders possessively. 'You're going to have hundreds of messages from just as many women.'

'Naturally, but also a few from my banker and my lawyer, and hopefully some from my few friends.'

'Why would your lawyer be calling you?'

'A minor problem.' He looked into the room behind her.

'What's wrong?' She felt furious towards this problem, as if it was a dog clinging to his clothing trying to bite him. For her he was the one sane and beautiful thing in the world, yet with a legal snap society's rabid power could yank him away from her.

He laughed, resting in her eyes. 'Nothing for you to worry about, my sweet blue one.' He caressed her cheek, frowning slightly as if trying to fathom just how deeply she felt for him.

'Won't you tell me?' She gazed up at him trustingly.

His lips curved up with the wicked air of a hunter's bow aiming a piercing stare into her heart's delicious tenderness, but then he looked away again. 'It's nothing serious, my love. Don't be concerned.' He slipped his hands under her short black dress.

'No, Jim, not now…'

'Yes, now…'

'No!' She laughed and ran into her bedroom. She saw her Dream Recorder and thought, *Oh, God, what am I going to do with all those dreams of Alex?* as Jim ran in growling and dove onto the bed with her. 'I thought you were going to call your answering service!'

'Oh, that's right.' He sat up.

'No, wait.' She pulled him back down.

'No, you're right.' He shook his head briskly, like a wet puppy. 'There's plenty of time for that later, we have to take care of business now, so let go of me.'

'But Jim…'

'No buts for now.' He smacked her ass and got up. 'By the way, don't bring your Dream Recorder, they make you lazy.'

'What? I love it.'

'Only conscious creativity will carve things out into reality.'

'Oh, Jim, I love it when you say things like that so quickly and so casually.'

He shrugged, exiting into the living room to use her phone,

and Elizabeth lay staring at her colorless walls, biting her lip to keep from remembering that one night with Alex. He had made her walls violet, and her dresser golden, and the door a dark forest-green... She rose quickly and examined her dream DVDs, distressed that she saw Alex's name everywhere but couldn't find Jim's anywhere. She had never dreamed with him, not until they began making love, and she hadn't been able to record her dreams in his home. *It doesn't matter, what I have with him is real.*

# Chapter Sixteen

Jim dropped Elizabeth off at her hideaway. He was going away for two days. He said he had financial matters to attend to, and her presence would only distract him. She sat on her couch after he left dreading that he would never return. He was so precious to her, there seemed no end to the things that could harm him, yet, paradoxically, she also felt he was invulnerable since her desire to live absolutely depended on him. *It's only for two day. Do something productive, for Christ's sake.*

She made herself get up but stopped in the middle of her living room as if on a ship's swaying deck and broke into a directionless weeping. For over a year, her life had been steered by the thought of him; he had never been out of her mind even when she felt she didn't love him. She realized now that she had depended on the atmosphere of his personality longer than she had cared to admit, and being separated from him now was almost unendurable, like not being able to breathe easily. She wondered then about the fact that she seldom thought of his past. It didn't have the power to upset or worry her as her reason said it should. In the month they had been together, she hadn't seen head or tail of other women. She sensed them still invisibly surrounding him like sirens, forever singing the alluring song of variety, but she didn't for a moment doubt the strength and virtue of her power over him.

He was bound to her now, and she knew it was for his soul's own good.

*My art supplies are here,* she thought, and ran to the closet. *I can create a beautiful scene for him to enter when he returns.'*

\* \* \*

By the following evening, Elizabeth had completed a 9x12 color drawing and felt wonderfully lighthearted anticipating the experience of Jim entering her imagination's realm. She sighed, gathering up the oil pastels and markers strewn around her on the wooden floor. She had been working at her glass coffee table, sitting cross legged like a child passionately bent over a coloring book. Spreading herself luxuriously back across the cool oak boards, she rested for a moment...

She got up and strolled to her CD player, smiling as she picked up a little golden sun containing Alex and his friends. She held it up to the light to see the rainbow arching within it, then fed it to the black machine. She pressed PLAY and her doorbells chimed an unexpected introduction to the music. She glanced out a window and noticed that the sun had set. Her mind as peacefully dark as the sky, she went and opened the door.

'Alex! What a coincidence, I just...' But she knew she didn't believe in coincidence and her heart plunged, a hopeless and heavy wishing stone, into his blue eyes. She stepped back quickly, but he walked inside.

'I was hoping you'd be here,' he said.

Her awareness flickered dangerously beneath his whisper; another second in his company and she wouldn't know what she was doing. 'Alex...' she began, but then her control crashed along with the drums in the music as he pulled her into his arms and his mouth came down over hers, their tongues irresistibly dancing together. She caressed his hair, which felt softer than the silence as the song ended. His hands slipped beneath her shirt, covering her breasts, and her head fell back weakly, all reason felled by the sharp pleasure of his touch.

'I've been dying to play you at least once more, Elizabeth,' he said, and this time his sexy whisper blew her mind. She barely noticed as he lifted her in his arms and carried her into her dark bedroom. He lay her on the edge of the bed with her legs hanging off the mattress like the slender necks of an instrument miraculously veined for his touch. 'There was such an intense harmony between us,' he went on quietly, but she barely heard him she was so intent on the feel of his hands stroking her legs and swiftly pulling down her panties. 'There was such a perfectly controlled rhythm between us...' He knelt between her legs and all thoughts vanished from her mind, drowned by the instant flood of joy she experienced as the solid wave of his tongue arched and dipped into her cunt. She gasped beneath a molten rush of sensations as his warm breath made her pussy even hotter for his sucking lips and twirling, teasing tongue. It was too late to stop him, but then a voice inside her cried, 'Jim!' and she opened her eyes...

Violet, red and green pastels and colored markers loomed before her face where her cheek rested on the oak floor boards. She sat up, dazed. The room was silent. She had only dreamed she got up and played Alex's music.

She rested her head on her arms on the glass table and cried from an exhausting and terrifying mixture of disappointment and relief.

# Chapter Seventeen

The large, double front doors were open in the oceanic hall and Elizabeth and Jim were greeting their guests. Holding hands, three couples entered one after the other as if in ceremonial procession, their fingers the grooves of two shells merged by countless waves of shared pleasure. Elizabeth knew only two of the persons, so Jim whispered their names to her as they approached.

First entered Mario and Audrey, her curly long hair the disheveled gold of autumn leaves framing dark, tropical green eyes. She was swathed in a long dress that glimmered different colors where the light hit it, so that she was never the same, a golden wave flowing over her full breasts, and then a red serpent slithering between her thighs, her curving figure fascinatingly alive. Her husband, Mario, taught poetry at Jim's school, and he led Audrey by the arm with a serious, sensitive pride that declared her body the living verse of his heart's rhythm and her soul his intimate poem of the world. He was tall and slender, his strong, refined features, broad shoulders and short black hair giving him the appearance of a Mayan priest in his white cotton shirt with colorful pyramids embroidered over the chest.

Mario and Audrey were followed by Steve, Jim's one-time bass player, and his wife Koto, like day and night. Steve's light-blue eyes and smoothed back icy blonde hair evoked a sunny

*Moonlit Dreams*

winter afternoon, the open folds of his white shirt the blank pages of a book he casually allowed you to fill with your own impressions as he signed it with his casual smile. His Japanese wife, Koto, possessed the silent quality of night. Her pitch-black eyes set in a pure white face made Elizabeth see deep pools in a royal winter garden under the full moon, her slender white limbs evoking snow-covered branches, yet the fire burning deep in the earth's core was still felt in the warm rose tone of her dress.

Jim had requested that his female guests wear long dresses to commence the enchanted weekend he had planned, and Elizabeth had chosen three boys from the school to act as each couple's personal page. The students were all dressed in black, as Jim had instructed them to be, and Michael, her favorite, was one of them. Every boy in the school had coveted the exciting honor of witnessing Jim's Dionysian festivity in honor of his engagement, but the three lucky ones seemed a little nervous now that they were actually there. They stood in silent orbit around Jim and Elizabeth until they were assigned a couple, then they shot like comets out to the car for their luggage, and returned to escort them upstairs.

Jim signed Michael to take charge of Steve and Koto, but Elizabeth said, 'No' and arrested the boy's eager stride. 'He's for Alex and Linda,' she said, and without comment, Jim waived Michael back, signing to Jeff instead as Steve and Koto slowly started up the stairs behind Mario and Audrey, careful not to break the procession even as they smiled over their shoulders. Jim's invitations had been mailed in the form of little booklets bound with flowering vines, leaves and petals cascading over his written commands:

> *No words on arriving at twilight*
> *only smiles reflecting the horizon*
> *then follow Adonis up to the sky*
> *and rise into One as the sun falls*

His friends seemed to enjoy obeying him, arriving with the regal air of Medieval nobles to a festivity that would last two nights and begin with a masked dance, stereo speakers strategically placed all through the house.

Finally, Alex and Linda approached, smiling. His golden hair had the same blinding effect on Elizabeth it always did. It rose like the sun over Linda's water-blue skirt, from which a thin black stem rose as if out of her navel and budded into silk green leaves clinging wetly to her breasts, her gentle waist and shoulders enticingly bare. She possessed delicate, well-defined features, her complexion was so clear it was almost luminous, and her light-brown hair hung straight and heavy as a waterfall down her naked back.

*So this is Alex's world.* Elizabeth smiled at them and signaled to Michael, infinitely grateful for Jim's rule of silence. The boy returned swiftly with a small red suitcase, and she watched the train of Linda's long, shimmering skirt flowing against gravity up the stairs, her round hips warm, life-filled oceans beside Alex's cool black leather universe.

Jim was also wearing black, but a belt of golden suns orbited his hips. Silently, they walked alone up to their own room, where she saw three Elizabeth's enter in a tight violet dress classically cut over one shoulder and slit on both sides up to her hips to reveal the elegant stride of her legs in star-patterned silver stockings.

'Kneel on the bed,' Jim commanded her softly.

She obeyed, waiting for him with her hair streaming around her face. She felt him unfasten his belt and get on the bed behind her, raising the curtain of her dress as he knelt behind her. Then she heard his hiss of pleasure when he discovered that her crotchless stockings were designed for him to take her wherever he desired that night without ruffling her sleek, catlike composure. She imagined Linda's blue skirt flowing like water through Alex's fingers, flooding his arms as he reached beneath it while Jim entered her with a slow, savoring appreciation… She saw Alex biting the tender bud of Linda's nipples through the silk green leaf as his erection slid in and out of her pussy faster and harder, her liquid hips almost instantly dissolving his hard-on as he climaxed…

'Oh, yes, Elizabeth!' Jim's fingers dug almost painfully into the tender flesh of her hips as he pumped his hips and his cum baptized the deepest darkest recesses of her pussy.

She moaned beneath the exquisite sensation of his cock throbbing between her thighs because with her eyes closed it was so easy to imagine it was Alex's pulsing erection drenching her innermost flesh with the salty depths of his pleasure…

'You're getting very good at squeezing my dick with your cunt,' Jim praised her crudely as he smoothed her dress back down and helped her off the bed.

'Thank you, my lord.' She avoided his eyes afraid he would see she had been thinking about another man as he fucked her.

# Chapter Eighteen

Jim donned his Zorro-like black mask and helped fasten her more slender, glimmering purple band. Their guests appeared to have followed directions and were all now in the dining room, pecking at the buffet like beautifully exotic birds idly stretching conversational wings. As their hosts entered, the notes of a guitar electrified the house, striking like lightning as drums rumbled, beating a massive heart in the darkness behind the candle flames' frail pulses. Jim stepped behind his large crystal bowl and everyone flocked around it on cue.

'Welcome, lords and ladies. Raise your goblets for the enchantment I brewed especially for this most magical, some had believed, impossible occasion – my engagement to the princess Elizabeth! Come now, two at a time.' He officiated over his alcoholic concoction with a priest's dignified air.

Elizabeth stepped shyly back into a dark corner as he filled everyone's glass, watching their guests disperse into the lounge, and it hurt her that Jim quickly poured his own drink and followed them without waiting to serve her or even looking to see where she was. Angrily, she walked up to the bowl, but before she had a chance to pick up the ladle, a black gloved hand reached for it from behind her. It was Alex who filled her glass.

'Thank you, my lord,' she said.

'My pleasure, princess.'

They laughed, and Jim smiled at them as they walked into the lounge together, which made Elizabeth hate him for a moment, then immediately long to be by his side, touching him, assuring herself of his love.

The women gathered together. Audrey reclined on a couch, her body a burning harvest of colors in the candlelight. It was sweet the way she kept smiling softly, as if she detected a pleasurable subtlety in the simplest statements, her long figure a flowing cursive expressing her confident and relaxed attitude towards life.

Koto sat at Audrey's feet, occasionally studying the other woman's costume jeweled sandals, curious yet self-contained as a Siamese cat and looking a bit frosty away from Steve's golden head and warm smile. Elizabeth was fascinated by the secretive narrowness of her eyes and her almost supernatural stillness, her slender arms wrapped around her bent knees giving her the appearance of an exquisite ancient statue brought uncertainly to life thousands of years from its own time. Elizabeth glanced at Koto's husband, laughing and talking freely, and felt that everything his wife didn't say was much more real.

Delightfully good-natured, Linda stood beside her hostess, more than once sipping her drink at the same moment she did, so that Elizabeth uncomfortably felt there was an invisible string connecting them. Linda didn't notice, but it made her feel as if her own personal worth was diminished; she got an inkling of what a concubine belonging to a great lord must have felt like in the presence of his royal wife. She was Jim's queen, but a small, lesser part of her would always mysteriously belong to Alex. She was contemptuously pleased that Linda seemed a bit superficial, laughing a lot and keeping the conversation flowing. She darted like a content robin from one topic to another, and Elizabeth was amused that Koto looked like a cat at once entertained and annoyed by her flightiness, and Audrey was the pleasant leaf-strewn ground on which they all met.

Elizabeth herself felt detached from the women; she was too preoccupied by the group of men on the other side of the room, desperate not to admit to herself how much the vision of Alex in a black mask and gloves affected her. The three of them were the only ones in full costume, and Jim looked so dangerous she couldn't concentrate on idle conversation. She was relieved when the female bouquet scattered as the punch began to hit and they were irresistibly drawn back to their mates.

Jim strode to the center of the room. 'Lords and ladies, we are now going to play hide and seek.'

Steve laughed. 'Who hides?'

'The women, of course, since that is their metaphysical nature, to be sought out, because part of them is always hidden. Naturally, we go after our own wife, so if we come across someone who doesn't belong to us, we simply move on. Are the rules understood, noble ones?'

'Perfectly,' Alex responded.

'Then listen well, lovely ones. We are now going to close our eyes, and in five minutes we will come after you.' Jim's voice rang dramatically in the charged space between songs.

Audrey grinned, Koto blinked a few times, and Linda laughed.

'Well, come on, move it, girls!' He fell into the chair behind him and closed his eyes.

'This is a silly game.' Koto's deep, quiet voice somehow carried over the music.

'I'll pretend I didn't hear that,' Jim said, then shouted, 'One, two, three, four…'

Steve gave Koto a gentle shove and the men dramatically closed their eyes as their wives all headed into the house. Elizabeth smiled and waved as she started alone into the yard.

It was a beautiful July night, warm and dry. Jim lived far from any street lights so the stars on her luminous hose seemed to be falling from the sky in the shape of legs and glimmering across the dark grass. She passed the bushes that had caught her dress the night they played Dracula's Castle. She knelt without thinking and spread herself across the cool grass behind the bushes. She lay there listening to leaves rustling in the breeze, her soul understanding what they were saying more clearly than words... *You love Jim and he loves you,* they explained peacefully. *When you're in the grave it's his embrace you will feel. The borders of heaven will be his arms and his kiss...* She sighed. *Alex is death...*

A man's black shoes paused beside her on the other side of the bushes concealing her, as though he could somehow distinguish her sigh from the breeze. Instinctively she knew it wasn't Steve or Mario. He started to move away, and suddenly she saw her arm stretch out, and when her hand grasped his ankle, she knew it wasn't Jim.

'Who's there?' he whispered, crouching down, and he saw her purple mask glittering beneath the leaves. 'Elizabeth!' he breathed, then he repeated her name again softly, 'Elizabeth...' as she kept a firm hold on his ankle.

'Meow, move on,' she whispered, expecting him to laugh and obey her but instead he looked around him, and the hunger in her blood dangerously flooded the dam of her reason.

*He's looking to see if anyone's there!* The words tumbled through her mind. *He wants me! He wants me!*

She let go of his ankle and grabbed his hand, sliding deeper under the bushes, and he followed her in as if hypnotized by her violet eyes. She rolled on top of him quickly, exquisitely pressed against him by the low-lying branches. His body was so different from Jim's, deep yet firm, and he didn't say anything, he didn't tell her what to do. He was hers, the grassy field of his chest there to plant with her desire. She fumbled with his belt and he helped her, unzipping his pants for her. Her mind went into vertigo, the living night around her centering on the feel of his penis as she pulled it out into her hand. She fell onto her side, desperately lifting her skirt up out of the way, and he rolled on top of her. She positioned him, stroking his stiffening cock as she filled the hungry mouth of her hole with his deliciously thick head. He penetrated her slowly, subliminally pausing to strike every possible note of joy along her smooth path as if it was the neck of one of his guitars, transforming her veins into strings playing out the breathless music of their pleasure. He sank all the way inside her before he began thrusting fast and hard because there was danger and not enough time. She didn't care at all about coming; she was too involved in the almost mystically soft feel of his hair beneath her fingers, too lost in the full, explosive warmth of him inside her and on top of her. Yet his swift, perfect rhythm carried her effortlessly along with him as they moaned quietly, desperately together, afraid of being heard. Then there was a gaspingly silent, infinite expansion between them, and he rolled off her as if unconscious.

She quickly zipped up his pants and buckled his belt. 'Go!' she whispered.

He kissed her, slid out from beneath the bushes, and she felt him run off.

\* \* \*

Elizabeth strolled back into the house nervously chewing on a blade of grass.

'Jim is still looking for you!' Audrey exclaimed, obviously proud of her for eluding him so successfully.

Elizabeth collapsed elegantly onto a black lounge, trying not to look at Alex. He was standing before the dark fireplace, one arm resting calmly on the mantle as the other restlessly whipped his mask off. 'Where the hell did you hide?' he asked, and she had to smile.

'She and Jim have probably played this game a hundred times, that's why she's so good at it,' Koto commented with barely concealed sarcasm.

'No we haven't,' Elizabeth responded coolly as Jim strode into the room and stopped dead.

'What are you doing here? You're not supposed to come out until I find you.'

'I would have been there forever,' she retorted.

'So what? You were supposed to wait for me to find you.'

'Well, how do you like that, I found myself.'

Everyone except Alex laughed as Jim strode over to her and she curled defensively up like a cat, gazing anxiously up at him.

'Did you have fun, baby?' he asked.

She felt his stare like a sword painfully inserting itself between her heart beats, and suddenly she understood the tale of Camelot because she was living it. She sat up, glancing at Alex as she thought, *It's the convent for me if I keep playing around like this*, and Jim seemed to read her mind. She could tell by the way his eyes widened looking down at her, conceivably making room for Alex in their bed.

'Did you have fun, baby?' he repeated.

'No, Arthur... I mean, Jim...' *My God, you fool, you just gave it away!* She started laughing.

'I think she had too much of your enchanted punch,' Mario commented.

'Poor Guenny, come here.' To her amazed joy, Jim pulled her up into his arms. They clung to each other passionately, desperately. She had never experienced such a cold, heavy darkening of her mind and body, as if for a moment the sun living in her blood had been forever shot down by the thought of losing him. 'So I'm you're king, am I?' he whispered.

'Yes! Forever!'

He pulled away from her slightly to address their guests. 'The king and queen are retiring to their chamber,' he announced. 'You lords and ladies may do as you please.'

# Chapter Nineteen

Once they were up in their room, Elizabeth couldn't look at Jim, but she observed the motion of his three reflections and their expressions trying to catch a hint of what he was really feeling. She couldn't bring herself to believe he wasn't upset or angry, that he had actually forgiven her for what she knew he suspected had happened between her and Alex.

She sat on the leather couch like a bad little girl in the principal's office waiting for her punishment, the severity of which she was sure was going to be in direct proportion to his relaxed attitude. But she didn't care, she deserved it. She sat with her hands crossed in her lap as he unmade the bed with a dangerous silence.

There was nothing in the room except his big white bed, a wooden night table, and the black couch she was sitting on merging with the shining black surface of the floor. There was no extraneous outside world in Jim's home, but especially in his room where the only law was whatever he desired; the only time the pulsing rhythm of his penetrations; the only weather the storm of their breathing and the rain of her tears as she sometimes cried from the intensity of the pleasure. In his bedroom there were only the warm desert tones of their naked flesh; the wet, dark cave between her legs; and the mysterious cocoon of his penis from which his spirit took flight in climax after climax. Their love was the entire world in this room, and tonight it felt like a dangerous, unknown shore beat on by the dark, powerful waves of blood flowing through his heart.

He approached her, his clam gaze in unnerving contrast to how fast her heart was beating. She didn't know what to say as she tried to convince herself that what was so arousing about Alex was the fact that they never really communicated except on a sensual level; they didn't really know each other and never really would. That was why climaxing with him had the absolute quality of dying, because there was no love between them to survive the explosion of their bodies. She didn't know if this was true or not, she only knew she had to make a choice, so she didn't say anything, returning Jim's gaze with a profound silence. He sat down beside her and she wanted to fling her arms around his neck and rest her mind against his heart, but she couldn't; she didn't deserve to be able to do so. She glanced at him, her hands still folded demurely in her lap, and he smiled kindly.

'I want to see you masturbate,' he said.

She was as momentarily shaken as if he had slapped her. She couldn't think and therefore didn't know how to feel. A weak little, 'Why?' was all she could manage staring down at her hands.

'Because I want you to,' he urged gently. 'Don't you want to please me?'

'Yes,' she whispered.

'Then masturbate for me.'

She squeezed her eyes shut for a moment, feeling absolutely trapped.

*Yes, I want to please him, but I don't want to do this. What a fucking devil he is, this is the perfect punishment.*

'But I won't feel anything,' she protested without conviction, knowing this was precisely his point.

'Sure you will,' he encouraged her in the quiet voice that

always hypnotized her. 'I'll be watching you. Come on...' He reached down and slowly raised her skirt, caressing her thighs as he did so. But when he reached her hands she wouldn't unclasp them, as if she was desperately praying. He pulled them apart. 'Come on!' He yanked her skirt down her legs and flung it away. 'Come on, baby...' He inserted his hand gently between her thighs. 'I'm going to give you something.'

He got up and walked over to the night table. His black-clad body was a deep moving shadow in the moonlit room, and she watched him with frightened wonder as he walked towards her again holding something long and ghostly-white in one hand. He sat down next to her again and held it up for her to look at before caressing her cheek with it. He was offering her an ivory shaft the length and width of a very large penis decorated with miniature raised carvings.

'You'll like it, trust me, baby,' he assured her in a sweet, cajoling tone, and to her dismay she felt herself becoming excited. She took the expensive stone dildo from him. 'That's my girl.' He sat back to watch her, and she saw his beautiful profile staring at her in the mirror across from them.

She spread her legs, and experienced a surprisingly exquisite suspense. But then she froze and looked at him desperately. 'Jim, I can't, it's too big...'

He clicked his tongue and shook his head. 'You're not trying very hard...' He reached down and gripped the end of the ivory shaft. 'Would it help if I held it?' he asked, staring into her eyes, distracting her. He smiled, and suddenly thrust the stone dildo inside her without warning, painfully forcing the smooth length past her dry labial lips into her moist interior.

'Oh, God!' she cried, and gripping the cold ivory cock tried pulling it out of her even as he kept pushing it in remorselessly.

'I'll let go if you promise to be a good girl and keep it inside you!'

'I promise!'

He sat back again and she stared at the ivory column emerging from her violet-netted mouth, its raised carvings stimulating her against her will. She thought of an ancient column emerging from the depths of humanity, her dark womb the living sphere of the night sky, the carvings on the shaft representing the time-line of human history mysteriously there for her stimulation...

She slowly slid the almost agonizingly hard dildo in and out of her reluctantly juicing pussy, falling into a sort of trance watching and experiencing its rhythmic motion. She pushed it in as deep as she could without losing her hold on it and felt as if she was descending to the beginning of the world touching the primeval cave wall of her womb...

She started to climax, slipping slowly down on the couch, moaning as she rubbed her clit with the fingertips of her right hand, morbidly burying the cold and massive dildo deeper and deeper into her belly until there was only a sphere like the full moon visible at the dark heart of her vulva.

'Oh, Jim...' She had almost forgotten his presence in her orgasmic trip through time inside her. He was staring at her with such a loving expression that a deep pain in her heart dissolved the cresting wave of the ecstasy. Whatever his defects in this mortal incarnation, they had no bearing on the radiant force of the being beside her she currently knew as Jim. His essence in his dark clothing was the life-filled darkness of the universe, and she felt she had emerged from him, the atmosphere her breath, the wind her sighs, the boundless ocean of life dammed between her thighs. They were all his, created just for him because the nature of her soul was his pleasure, she was nothing without him, her emotions an empty web without the spider it was designed to feed.

'My God!' she breathed. 'What did you put in that punch? I've never been so out there... I love you, Jim!'

He smiled and gently pulled the ivory dildo out of her pussy, laying the aside the shaft shimmering with her juices. 'Let me finish you off.' He flung her legs onto the couch so that she fell back across it. He arched his body over hers as she removed the belt of suns orbiting his hips and drew the dimensional column of his penis out from the black space of his pants. His cock was firm yet wondrously tender and warm, in divine contrast to the cool, hard ivory.

He dove into her pussy. 'Oh, God, Elizabeth, I love you!' He kissed her hungrily, angrily.

'I worship you, too!' she gasped. 'I would let you kill me!'

'I promise I will one day.'

Yet a few minutes later they were lying unharmed in each others arms on the bed. They lay there peacefully for a while, then he entered her again naturally, gently, and they rocked together, his body lying comfortably on top of hers. They licked each others lips, cheeks and neck, falling into a long, deep kiss every now and then, all the while their bodies maintaining a slow, steady rhythm. Elizabeth was filled with joy, because they had never made love like this, with such calm tenderness, lapped by gentle waves of pleasure that seemed endless, as if they could literally go on like this forever. She remembered what he had said about heaven being pure white sheets filled with the all-surrounding warmth of a lover, and she felt then that it was true. She might have been dead she was so absolutely free of discomfort and so exquisitely merging with him.

'Do you like this, sweetheart, soft and slow?' he whispered.

'Hmm, yes… don't talk…'

'Why?' He was looking down at her.

'Because… I lose control when you talk to me…'

He smiled and rubbed his cheek against hers like a cat. 'What's the difference between humans and animals, Elizabeth?' he asked conversationally.

'What?' She laughed.

He suddenly quickened his pace.

'No, Jim!'

'Then answer me.' He kept looking down at her and his direct stare was as arousing to her as his penetrations.

'You know what the difference is...' she began, concentrating on the answer to distract herself from the growing intensity of the pleasure. 'Animals don't wear clothes or jewelry.' She smiled.

He thrust hard once, both punishing her and rewarding her for this answer. 'But people started to wear clothes because they were cold.'

'No...' She caressed his legs with her feet, not wanting him to enter her too deeply, keeping it deliciously light. 'Civilization originated in the warmth of Africa, people didn't need clothes for protection, dressing was a religious thing, the bright colors and flowing patterns reminding them of what it was like in the spirit realm, because you see, the soul had just descended into a body and found it rather drab...'

He laughed beneath his breath, reaching back and pulling her legs up. 'That's how architecture got started, too,' she continued desperately, but his face was buried in her neck, his breathing was becoming uneven, he wasn't listening, 'as houses for the dead, shapes to help the ascent of the soul and protect it from being dispersed by the wind and the elements...' Her body began chasing a climax. 'Jim, you're not listening!'

'Yes, I am... soul architecture... oh, yes... torn apart by the elements... Oh, Elizabeth...'

'Now do you understand what clothing has to do with being human? It's the energy of the soul creating its own form and descending into it...'

'Yes, baby, I got it... I got it... tell me more...'

'No... I can't...'

Yes, come on... I want to hear more about the soul descending into form... Oh, yes, I do!'

'Oh, God, I worship you! Harder! Harder!'

'Descending into form... torn apart by the elements... animals don't wear jewelry... Why? Tell me why!'

'Because... jewels stand for magical concepts felt by the soul like precious gems are worn by the body!'

'Oh, God, Elizabeth, you don't stop, baby! I can't get enough of you! And now I'm going to come inside you.'
'Oh, yes, please, please, I want to come with you!'

# Chapter Twenty

It was afternoon. Everyone was lying out by the pool, and Elizabeth was exhausted by the effort of avoiding the sight of Alex almost naked in a blue swimsuit that stunningly matched his eyes. Jim and Mario were enjoying a heated discussion on the origin of the universe and the nature of God, while Alex and Steve amiably discussed the latest wonders in electronic musical equipment, and the women sunbathed in silence. They were all wearing sexy thong bikinis except Elizabeth, who preferred her modest one-piece.

She cried out, opening her eyes as someone dive-bombed into the pool and splashed water all over her hot body. She caressed the wonderfully cool liquid over her arms and legs. Emerging so suddenly from the dark recesses of her thoughts, the sunny day seemed to explode on her senses. The flawless blue of the sky made her think of the Virgin Mary's pure and radiant robes. It was Jim who had subjected her to a cleansing, and she watched now as he mischievously dunked Koto's ink-black head beneath the water.

Suddenly, Alex seated himself on the edge of her deck chair.

She returned his open gaze uncertainly, looking to make sure that Linda was still lying on her stomach with her face turned away.

'I have to tell you something, Elizabeth.'

*Oh, my Lord, Jesus Christ!* 'Yes, Alex?'

'That night at the restaurant... Jim set the whole thing up. I wasn't just there by chance, Elizabeth. He had told me you were obsessed with me. He said you were wearing me as some sort of ideal armor against any possible real relationship, and that unless I became flesh and blood to you and you got me out of your system you would never see that he loved you, and that you loved him. So, he asked me to meet you and to spend time with you later in order to disenchant you. You see, he trusted me, he had no idea I would... I was just supposed to look at your paintings while you realized I was just a normal married man, not your living dream man, but instead I took advantage of your feelings...'

Her heart raced joyously with Jim's swimming figure. *He loved me! All that time he loved me! He knew everything that was going through my mind and he loved me! Oh, God, what a beautiful fucking devil he is! I could kill him!* 'I'm so glad you told me this, Alex. Thank you.'

He returned her smile with his lips, but his eyes were sober. 'Then you'll undo the spell?'

For Elizabeth, the whole day darkened with his eyes.

'Even though it's my fault for betraying a friend's trust?'

Jim abruptly rose out of the pool and shook his soaking head over both of them. 'Cool it,' he commanded.

'It was very special, thank you,' Alex said to her, then returned Jim's stare for a steady moment before getting up and diving into the pool himself, so that Elizabeth felt like a priceless treasure at the changing of the guard.

'What was that all about?' Jim demanded.

'That was the end.' She lay back and closed her eyes, smiling peacefully.

\* \* \*

The world was grey and heavy outside the windows and behind her eyes on a cold Saturday morning in August.

'Jim, I'm depressed.'

They were still lying in bed. She stretched, and he flung the sheet away to watch her.

He bit one of her nipples gently. 'I'm going to turn one of the rooms in the east wing into a painting studio for you.' He kissed her stomach, spreading her legs. 'Mm, breakfast...' he murmured against her sex, crouching comfortably between her thighs.

She sighed, caressing his soft long hair, and after a moment he paused in his tongue's avid worship of her sleepy clitoris, gazing across the undulating landscape of her body into her eyes. 'Why are you so sad, sweet one?' He spread himself beside her again and took her in his arms. 'Do you miss Alex?'

'Oh, God, Jim, please!'

'I'm sorry.' He held her tightly.

She responded passionately. 'I love you so much, Jim. If anything happened to you, it would be the end of the world for me.'

'Well, this world is only one in a million trillion.'

'It would be the end of the whole universe.'

'Yes, but they say this is only one of infinite possible universes.'

'Fuck what they say! You're all of them.'

He laughed and kissed her for a long time, his tongue wandering lazily in her mouth perfumed by her pussy juices. 'Okay, baby,' he said at last, but I'm still here, so why are you depressed?'

'I don't know...'

'Come on, what are you thinking?' He smiled watching thoughts race as subliminal glints of light through her dark eyes. 'You know you can tell me, Elizabeth.'

'I know, it's just that I don't really know what's wrong... All I know is that if I lose you, I won't want to live.'

He held her close again. 'There's my baby,' he whispered. 'You're so beautiful. Just remember that I love you more than anyone on this planet.'

'I know, just don't let anything to happen to you, please.'

'I won't, don't worry, but if something does, you know I'll come back and fuck you as lightning.'

'Oh, Jim, please...'

He rolled onto his back and stared up at her reflection. 'I'll see what I can do...'

'What do you mean?'

'I know how you feel, but you shouldn't be so afraid of death, Elizabeth, it'll only be a temporary separation, and as Houdini said to his wife, I'll find a way to reach you.'

'I don't believe in that,' she said fervently. 'Only evil or lower level spirits use another's body to communicate through. And Houdini never did manage to get through to his wife.'

'I promise I'll be more sophisticated. Besides, no other body would suit me, I'm much to pleased with this one, and once it's gone I'd rather be naked energy. I fancy the idea of getting off as lightning, so that every time you heard thunder you'd know it was my groans of pleasure as I penetrated the earth below with my hot bolts.'

She laughed.

'I'm glad you feel better. You're hopelessly metaphysical, Elizabeth. All I have to do is talk cosmic for a minute, and you lighten up.'

'I guess that's the way I'm wired.'

'Yes, and how it turns me on! I'm looking forward to the next dimension. Just think what fun it'll be to travel in. You won't need suitcases, or restaurants on every corner. However, I'm not anxious to leave just yet, so I'll see what I can do about assuaging your restlessness on this plain.'

'It's just that, sometimes, I wish I could create not with paints but with energy... three-dimensionally fashion a world around us...'

'Uh huh.'

'I'm serious.'

'I know you are, sweetheart. You'll be a blast to be dead with, and like I said, I'm looking forward to it, but not today.'

# Chapter Twenty-One

A week later at dinner, Elizabeth was staring into a candle flame still unable to believe that Jim was everything she had ever dreamed. She told him how much she loved him all the time, yet the word couldn't possibly convey what she felt; it was like scattering bread crumbs before a winged angel of God he was so wise and beautiful in her eyes. The small flame pulsated gently, responding to the subtle, invisible currents of the moment while burning with an immutable intensity. *This is my body now, this candle slowly disintegrating... the wick is my spinal cord, the first thing that forms in an embryo.* She had seen films shot by micro cameras in the womb which showed what looked like a bright cluster of stars merging into a snake-like form, out of which the heart mysteriously began beating...

She nearly choked as Jim gripped her face and shoved a fork-full of food into her mouth. 'Eat,' he commanded. 'What the hell are you and that candle talking about, anyway?'

She raised her wine glass. 'A toast.'

He touched his glass to hers.

'Here's to my never disobeying you,' she said, 'unless you want me to. Yet I suppose that would still be obeying you, so here's to my doing only what you desire.' She finished her wine and stared down at the reddish black dregs feeling strangely powerful, like her soul gazing at the remains of one of its cremated bodies.

'What if I want you to do what you want to do?' He pushed his plate away.

'All my life I've waited for you, which means all I have left to want is what you want,' she replied. It excited her entering the slippery maze of language, because what they were thinking could become dangerously lost to each other if they didn't find just the right way to say it, and the goal was for their feelings to embrace at the conclusion. 'I am the embodiment of your every desire, so all I truly need, apart from the obvious creature comforts, is your fulfillment.'

He was silent, his features above the candles carved out almost sinisterly, his intense expression a supernaturally motionless fire that sent a hot rush of fear through her she enjoyed.

'But, actually,' she continued, smiling, 'I'm perfectly selfish, really. I want to be completely possessed by you, but if you didn't have the power to do it, it follows that I wouldn't want what you want, so, ultimately, I want what I want, even if that happens to be absolutely pleasing you, because – metaphysically, mind you, this is not an insult – you're even more divinely selfish than I am.'

He smiled a little.

'Deep down, you feel that everything is yours, that it all exists for your experience and pleasure as you mysteriously develop your conscious powers. But if you aren't true to your positive creative spirit, if you dim your force with fears or cynical, lazy compromises, it's in my nature to start denying you my favors…'

He stood up. 'Let's go.'

\* \* \*

They cuddled together in a deck chair on the balcony beneath the stars. He seemed to be thinking intently about something, but she'd had enough wine to merely enjoy absorbing his warmth as his absentminded caresses half hypnotized her. She had just slipped into a deep, dark peace when he sat up abruptly and jerked her painfully up with him. 'Get up!' he pulled her violently out of the chair.

'Are we going to sleep?' she asked hopefully.

He shoved her down onto her knees. 'No, you're going to please me now, oh embodiment of all my desires.'

She didn't feel she had the energy, but she supposed she deserved this, so she set about the task and his response pleased her so much she forgot she was tired, the hard, warm length of his erection against her cheeks and between her lips contrasting invigoratingly with the cool night air. But then all she could do was concentrate on not choking as he moved his big, pulsing cock quickly in and out of her mouth, shoving his head selfishly down into her throat.

'You worship me, don't you?' he asked, clutching her hands so she couldn't control the relentless rhythm of his hips, and her only desire was to keep his passage smooth, to not scrape him with her teeth and hurt him. 'Don't you?' he demanded, and she squeezed his hands in response, sucking passionately on his head. 'Oh, Jesus... you have me, Elizabeth, you've got me, baby...' Beneath the porch light it looked as if some of the distant, glimmering stars were falling onto her tongue as he jacked off, holding her firmly by the hair with his free hand.

After he finished coming, forcing her to swallow the entire microcosmic universe of his moment's pleasure, he pulled her up tenderly when he saw that her legs were stiff from kneeling. 'You know why you're so wise?' he asked. 'Because you swallow so much of my sperm.'

She laughed. 'I was wise before, that's why you fell in love with me,' she pointed out.

'I know.' He hugged her warmly. 'You *are* Isis,' he whispered. 'You really are, that's why it's probably not fair that I want you all to myself. Don't you think Alex deserves a goddess, too?'

'Jim!' She pushed him away.

'No, no, baby, don't get upset.' He pulled her back into his arms. 'It's just that sometimes I wonder if being allowed to take one sip made your thirst for him even worse...'

'Jim, why are you saying this?'

'Because it's true.'

'No!' She wrenched herself free of him and ran furiously into the house.

He caught her an instant later, turning her to face him, and her white dress flew away like foam beneath his hands as he yanked it up over her head. He ripped off her delicate lace panties and lifted her leg to rub his cool dry leather crotch against her wet pussy, his belt buckle cruelly branding her. Then he pulled her out onto the balcony again and lifted her onto the railing.

'Oh, no, Jim!' She buried her face in his neck as he unzipped his pants again and shoved his still erect cock up inside her with one determined thrust, her resistance falling into the darkness behind her, slipping away on his smooth rhythm...

Later that night something woke her. She saw her face staring down and up at her, confused for a moment as to whether she was still in her body or hovering over it in a dream, then she noticed Jim kneeling beside her on the bed. Without a word he pushed her over and fucked her from behind, using her so roughly she found herself imagining she was buried in the soft ground and slowly, exquisitely decomposing beneath his hungry bites and thrusts.

# Chapter Twenty-Two

Elizabeth was at her hideaway; Jim was with Steve somewhere, no doubt sharing idealized memories of road life as they got elegantly wasted. She lay on her couch all morning, now and then attempting to read but unable to concentrate. Her mind felt light and hazy as smoke over the constant smoldering arousal of her body. They made love so often and so creatively all other activities seemed dull as ashes in comparison. She stared at her slender vase, made of shining blue glass, and felt blissfully weightless, like a genie who had emerged from it to give him his every wish, thus fulfilling her own nature. She wished she could slip down into the vase's cool, curving form and rest for a while inside it. Eventually, she got up to fix herself some lunch – a grilled cheese sandwich and a beer – then wandered aimlessly around the small living room, still reluctant to admit why she was really there.

*Don't do it.* It seemed an unhealthy desire to want to spend an afternoon alone watching the old fairy tales of her subconscious, but, of course, it's fun to do what one shouldn't. She was in her bedroom inserting a DVD into the Dream Recorder before she could stop herself. More than ever the black machine looked like a crouching shape about to leap out at her. She hadn't seen it in so long it scared her a little in the dark room. Red controls flashed evil eyes as she turned the power on, and against all her better judgment lay back across the bed, exultantly giving herself up to the questionable nature yet mysterious power of her own fantasies...

Church bells somberly tolled the hour of midnight as he beat their slow, deep rhythm into her, a raven invisibly perched on the pointed roof of her small house spreading its wings and echoing her cries as she climaxed in his arms. It was as if the only light inside her was his golden hair, her thoughts the shadows from the fire caressing him, concerned only with possessing him as he rose from the bed. He had a wife and a child to protect, he could never return, and he demanded she give him back his soul. She lay enjoying the comforting touch of the fire in the absence of his body, smiling. 'It is they who would steal it from you,' she replied. 'It is safe with me.'

'You are a witch,' he murmured. 'They will burn you.'

She shook her head. 'You will not tell them.'

Dressed now, he sat on the narrow bed beside her, and her hands slipped eagerly beneath his shirt's rough cloth. He did not stop her...

From the darkness outside she rose as if from a grave into another dream, the white silk lining of her coffin the icing of an eternal birthday wedding cake – her forced marriage to Death, the candles around her forever burning how old she was when He took her. She sat up inside an open coffin wearing a white gown, tiny red buttons lining the bodice like frozen drops of blood, a spidery black shawl trailing behind her as she left the crypt, passing silent as a patch of moonlight through the church yard towards the Manor where he lived – the man she still desired even though her kiss was death to him and meant eternal damnation for her. She entered his room through glass doors, hiding for a moment within the purple velvet curtains bleached violet by the moonlight in which all her feelings still vibrated. She approached the cloud of his bed where he floated in a dream she could not see, and slowly lifted the sheet like mist from the warm plains of his naked body. Swiftly she spread the webbed shadow of her shawl over his chest, and he awoke as her spider hands crawled over him hungrily, her pulse coming back to life through the mingled fear and desire in his eyes. His neck looked to her like the most delicious substance growing on earth beneath the fine golden rays of his hair, a strand for every day she had lived and hundreds more to sustain her now as her sense of self resurrected in the heaven of his eyes. He closed them, avoiding the sight of his death, but his hands rose to blindly caress her. She realized then that soon his body would be a cold weight in her embrace, his heart that was beating so swiftly a dead bird in her hands, and for her the world would vanish with him... the sky would forever darken as his eyes closed, his hair still shining but coldly, like the sun on an endless winter day, his stiff form descending into the earth's darkness... yet still she couldn't stop herself. His hot blood sprang eagerly against her tongue, each drop quivering with the rhythm of his heartbeats, and his helpless moans intoxicated her beyond control. She stroked his cock as she sucked his blood and felt his desire growing even as his body weakened. She desperately resisted the urge to drain him. She wanted to return every night, to sip and savor his unique flavor, so she drew her teeth gently out of his neck just as the door of the bedroom opened behind her. She leapt off the bed and hissed wildly as Jim approached her. She looked from the moonlit panes of the glass doors to the gleam of the knife in his hand. Both possessed a shattering power that attracted her and weakened her with indecision, so that she pressed herself back against a wall as he moved towards her. He was wearing a white shirt with delicate ruffles over the chest that enhanced the determined set of his mouth, and suddenly, more than she thirsted for Alex, she longed to follow the direct path of his stare embodied in the naked blade for she understood that he wanted to save her. If she let him embrace her he would deliver her from the grave's hopeless lust. She ran past him towards the doors, and he fulfilled her terrible inner hunger as he caught her against him and thrust the dagger straight into her heart...

The dream ended, yet once again she was seeing his white shirt as he entered the dark bedroom. She gasped, sitting up and clutching the dress over her heart.

'That sounded quite interesting.' His quiet voice only enhanced her sense of unreality as he stood in front of the blank screen, sinisterly silhouetted by its ghostly light. 'Would you mind if I saw it?'

She got up.

'Where are you going, Elizabeth?'

'I'm thirsty...'

She didn't return to the bedroom as she heard her vampire dream replaying, and after her death cry, she waited. He joined her in the kitchen, and they stood silently staring at each other for so long that the sound of a drawer opening beneath his hand was significantly ominous. He smiled coldly as he closed it to open another one and she stepped back, realizing what he was doing just as he pulled out a large knife. She stared at the blade, which she felt dividing her strangely in half – she became tense with fear, yet also strangely languid. He approached her, and shock pressed her back against the wall because she noticed that her short white dress was lined with tiny red buttons in the front just like her dream gown.

'Jim...'

'Don't move.' He spoke quietly, preserving the moment's dreamy aura as he touched the bottom button of her dress with the tip of the knife. She held her breath as he followed the red trail, then gently scratched the bare flesh of her chest up to her throat, pinning her head back so she was forced to look at him. Fear and guilt made her avoid his eyes. He knew she had been watching her dreams with Alex, and so deserved to be punished... He cut her dress in half from the top down with a swift and terrifying exactness. The garment fell limply open, exposing her soft breasts, and she moaned as he drew the cloth back and touched one of her nipples with the knife's sharp tip.

'Jim...'

He rested the edge of the blade against the tender flesh joining her neck and shoulder. She felt a keen, burning sensation, and saw the cool metal stained with her blood as he held it up before her. Pain began its swift, deep throb through her body, yet, because she felt she deserved it, she somehow enjoyed it. *He is my master*, she thought, and went limp as he pulled her away from the wall and held her against him. *He is my lord!* He rested the flat of the blade against her spine and began sucking the blood from her cut.

'Oh, yes!' she breathed. 'Hurt me... hurt me more!' She wasn't at all sure it was wise to provoke him, but she couldn't help herself.

He raised his head, staring down into her eyes for a long moment before stepping back and holding the knife dangerously between them while he kept sucking her blood. The sharp sensation in her navel and the deep ache in her neck fused into a violent desire, so that when his free hand clutched one of her breasts she made to pull him to her.

'Elizabeth!' He quickly flung the knife away. 'Jesus Christ!'

\* \* \*

They lay side by side on her bed, Elizabeth tensely waiting for him to speak, her soul suspended like a ballerina on tiptoe depending on the choreography of his thoughts and feelings. The longer he remained silent, the more her emotions ached from the strain of wondering what he was thinking. She defended herself by shifting some of the blame onto him – if he hadn't accused her of still desiring Alex she wouldn't have come to her apartment today to be angrily unfaithful to him with her old dreams.

'Elizabeth, do you think we should have a child? It might mellow us out a little.'

'What?!' She sat up. 'Are you kidding?'

He smiled and pulled her back down. 'Yes, I just wanted to see how you would react. I thought that after almost stabbing yourself you might be possessed by the desire to affirm your life by creating another one, thus assuring yourself of some sort of normal longevity, because good mothers and fathers don't play with kitchen knives.'

'I'm too selfish to have children, and I would be jealous if it was a little girl and you were always paying attention to her. Besides, I would always remember that they were little adults who would one day grow up and leave us to live their fantasies just like I did, so I'd rather fulfill myself completely than spend the best part of my life raising other people who'll just leave to live their own lives when the time comes. I don't have a maternal bone in my body,' she concluded.

'But if I broke one, it might set differently.'

She laughed, slipping her arms around his chest, corralling the wild beauty of his heart for herself. She was so grateful that he didn't seem upset. Perhaps he realized she had only been watching her dreams because she was angry at the way he had behaved the other night.

'How would you define the soul, Elizabeth?'

'Awareness of our creative power and responsibility as the manifest heart of God.'

'Very good. Did you just come up with that this minute?'

'Yes.'

'A plus, even though I don't believe in God.'

'Lets not get into that now. I don't believe in a bearded entity either; that's not what I mean by God and you know it.'

They held each other in silence for a while.

'Jim, do you believe in soul mates? What do you think happens when we die?'

'Do you mean, "Is heaven a divine orgy where I can have both you and Alex?"'

' Jim!' She was angry again. 'Stop this! Why do you keep bringing him up? He doesn't mean anything to me. That dream just happened to come one. I just played a DVD at random,' she lied. 'Please don't think…'

'It's okay, Elizabeth, it turns me on that you're a bad girl.'
'Jim, be serious.'
'What can be more serious than what turns me on?'
'I don't want you to think...'
'I'm sorry I ruined your dress.'
'Don't change the subject.'
'I really liked that dress, too.'
'Jim...'
'I'll buy you another one just like it.'
'I hate you!'

He leaned over her and slapped her. 'You'd like me to beat him out of you, wouldn't you?' he whispered.

'Yes...'

'Fine, but not tonight. I need a drink.' He got up. 'Do you have any other clothes here?' He pulled open her closet. 'Not this one or this one... this one!' He flung the dress at her.

# Chapter Twenty-Three

A golden snake wound swiftly over the dirt road like a streak of sunlight in the hot, bright day. She smiled watching it pass, unafraid because she knew it belonged to the sorcerer who was her friend and mentor. He was teaching her the mysteries of nature so she could use them to capture whatever lord she desired. Years ago, when she was thirteen, he had stolen her from her village and brought her to live with him in a large, moss-carpeted cave. That night he had cruelly taken her virginity, causing her as much pain as possible and offering it to the forest in exchange for some of its hidden power, which he sealed inside her with a long, deep kiss afterwards. The following night he made her lie naked beside a fire at the mouth of the cave as he talked to her and fucked her at the same time, the wind punctuating his statements on the nature of magic with sparks that burned a mysterious sense into her beyond the obvious pain. 'Your spirit is the eternal space in which the conscious fire of your soul burns, using different limbs each life time…' Thus he spoke, and at dawn he possessed her again, but gently this time, so that she first tasted pleasure when the sun appeared behind the trees, the world growing more and more luminous as ecstasy was born inside her. He gave her a new name then, whispering it in her ear as she climaxed. He said this was her true birthday and that she was to forget her first one and all the circumstances surrounding it the way she would forget her skeleton in the grave when she died. After that morning she willingly responded to her new name and obeyed him.

They walked through the forest during the day, setting and checking traps as he taught her his secrets and introduced her to some large old trees that were good friends of his. He said trees always understood you, whereas other humans seldom did. 'And they're completely selfish without hurting anyone, which is already an amazing achievement.'

'Why do you say trees are selfish?'

'Because, they do nothing but create leaves to feed themselves to grow more branches, and seeds to grow more trees. There is no rational purpose for their existence, only the joy they take in their own being, which is so great it provides a home and nourishment for countless other living things. Humans who create beautiful things, whether it be a painting, or a poem, or a goblet, are nourishing themselves with the power of the divine as a tree feeds on sunlight when it sprouts leaves; and the more joyously creative they are, the happier is everyone who absorbs the exhalation of their imagination for their own growth.'

He told her that most herbs stood for specific human emotions and thus had a medicinal effect on the vital organs, which symbolized the soul's conceptual functions as an incarnate, self-experiencing energy. He said the forest was an extension of her body and that the different creatures within it could help her understand the magical nature of her perceptions.

'Take, for example, the falcon. It embodies man's ability to soar in the realm of thought and conceive of heaven, sensing the powerful freedom of the spirit behind his reasoning like the wind beneath a bird's wings. The wolf, on the other hand, is the force of his sensuality, the darkness inside him concerned only with its self experience that also destroys, with the relentless teeth of death and decay, the very form it nourishes itself on.'

She wanted to know more about herbs and how they related to her feelings, so they walked a little way until he found a mandrake root. 'This is a man's sex.' He exposed his own organ. 'Feel them both at once.'

She obeyed him, observing how his was soft while the root felt invulnerably hard. He instructed her to wash the mandrake in a stream. 'Now suck on one and then the other…' She willingly obeyed him again, and her mind darkened strangely, until she felt as if she was nothing but a vast mouth holding him and the root inside her, the rhythm of moving from one to the other swiftly blurring so that their experience seemed simultaneous. 'You are the world in which we are,' she heard him say as if from a long way away, 'that is the pure nature of your being.'

She looked up at him. 'I prefer you to the root,' she observed.

He laughed. 'Naturally, for I create myself and the mandrake is only my reflection in the mirror of water from which physical life emerged as a result of my spirit gazing at itself. And you, my dear, are the witch who is holding that mirror up for me, and if you understand this, when you fondle the root you also caress my soul.' He helped her up off her knees. 'One day you will see the man for whom your heart is beating the day and night of this world. I will teach you a drink you can make of this root to give him so he feels a great peace illuminating his heart and a serpent of fire coursing through his blood. Thus you will have begun the integration of heaven and earth with your love.'

'But I want only you!' she exclaimed.

He did not respond to this but simply began explaining other herbs to her – jealousy, fear, tenderness, discontent, violence, tranquility – there seemed no end to the range of emotions in the forest's body. 'A true man consciously embraces the world's mystery so his soul is healthy and whole and he rules his emotions like a lord his vassals, not letting them get the better of him but rather using them to deepen the fertility of his being and strengthen his heart's divine fortress.'

'There are few real men, are there not?'

'Yes, alas.'

Late one afternoon she was wandering alone collecting her favorite berries and she came closer than she ever had before to the dirt path winding between the trees which she knew led to man's world. She remembered from her youth in the village, and knew from the things her mentor had told her, that most men lived life full of fear and doubt and were constantly fighting each other because they did not know how to truly enjoy themselves, so she had no desire to encounter any of them. The setting sun seemed to explode off each wet leaf, and it was as if the streams were rushing between the banks of her thighs she felt so wonderfully alive. That day she was not afraid of the road, instead it excited her that she would be punished for venturing to close to it. Then, miraculously, she saw the setting sun gently pulsing towards her between distant branches. After pausing in awe a moment she ran towards it eagerly, hiding behind a large oak tree that sent large roots across the forbidden path. 'One day, you will see the man for whom your heart is beating the day and night of this world...' The words rang in her head in rhythm with the horse's hooves, the rich purple saddle cloth draping the black animal approaching her like the dark gleam of dusk on the horizon. She wanted that cloth more than anything until she saw the gold of the rider's long hair waving over an open white shirt, his sweat glistening with a radiance that blinded her. He was riding at a slow trot, relaxed in the saddle, and she was not afraid that night was following swiftly behind him, as if his golden head had the power to protect her in the sun's absence. She stepped lithely out onto the road and his horse reared to a stop. She caressed the animal's warm muzzle reassuringly, whispering in its ear, 'You will ride with your master through many beautiful places if you always bring him back to me.' She looked up at the man, barely able to make out his features beneath the tree's deepening shadow, but his hair still shone and his presence was so intense it weakened her. 'Dismount,' she commanded, 'your horse is not going anywhere until I tell him to.' She clutched her lilac cloak around her and took confident root as she let her feelings waft curiously around him, caressing him with the breeze as she stood perfectly still beneath him.

'Then release him,' he said, but his voice was kind.

'Why?' She hid her despair, for she knew she could not disobey him yet she did not wish him to leave.

He was silent.

'Why?' she repeated, the wind playing with her long black hair. 'Come with me,' she lifted a hand to him, 'and be free...' Her arm emerged pale and slender as a concentrated beam of moonlight from her cloak, exposing the shadowy curve of a breast she felt instantly fill his mind; easily conquering the tough weed of his rational resistance with its sensual bloom. He dismounted, but kept hold of his horse's reins. 'He will be safe here behind this tree,' she promised. 'He belongs to my dream now, and we must all ride our own, so no one will see him.' She walked quickly and lightly ahead of him into the forest, her cloak flying open and her heart beating swift as a bird's wings as she thought of all the wonders she could show him. She heard branches breaking beneath his stride and breathed a swift spell in which they stood for all the adverse circumstances that could come his way, giving him the power to crush them all. From that moment on, everything would serve only to feed and strengthen his soul's fire. She ran behind him and collected some of the twigs along his trail. After she had gathered an arm-full, she dropped them at his feet. 'If you smile, I can start a fire,' she told him.

'Just with a smile?'

She felt his amusement like a spark in the night. Quickly she touched his lips with her fingertips. 'Stand back...' She then touched the branching circumstances at his feet and a tiny flame licked up like a snake's tongue.

'How did you do that?' He looked closely at the growing fire, making sure it was real.

'Every time you smile, your soul shoots off a spark,' she explained. 'All I did was capture it.'

'How?' His features rose slowly out of the darkness beneath the swiftly spreading fire, and their clean lines licked hotly over her heart, the experience of his face utterly consuming her.

'With my love,' she whispered, her voice hiding with an unusual reluctance deep in her throat.

'How can you possibly love me?' He smiled again. 'You do not even know me.'

'I simply transferred the feeling I got from your smile into the wood.'

'What?' He laughed and the fire leapt.

'See! The wind is your spirit's breath, and I am the fire that lives inside you.' She stepped around the blaze and rested her hand on his sex. 'This is the wholeness that was and is...' He did not move away, so she began caressing his crotch. 'And as it feels itself, suns are born, and from them worlds, for your pleasure is my nature...'

He pushed her away gently. 'No.'

'Why?'

'You are lovely, but I cannot stay with you.'

'Why?'

'Because I have a wife whom I love.'

'But I do not wish to take you away from her, only to show you beautiful things.' She raised her chin proudly as she let her lilac cloak slip off her shoulders and faint to the ground at her feet. Shadows from the fire licked passionately up her naked body, hauntingly consuming it at the same time that they enticingly offered it to him, her beauty the pulsing heart of the tree-veined forest.

'What is your name?' he asked.

She twirled around the fire, her arms rising and undulating as she spun swiftly over to him and crashed against his chest. 'I am a spark! Catch me!' She flew away, picking up her cloak and trailing it behind her. 'Follow me into whatever dream you please!' She ran towards him again and flung the cloak over his head, pushing him down across the ground as, blinded, he lost his balance. She knelt beside him, smoothing the cloth over him and firmly grasping his hands so he couldn't remove it. 'Be still!' she whispered forcefully. 'Imagine my cloak as the mist of any realm you wish to visit, the cloud of any world you can conceive and water with your imagination. Make a wish!'

He lay still.

'Have you wished?'

'Yes, and it won't be hard to grant.'

She rested her cheek against his heart. 'Tell me.'

'I wish for what I already have. What more could I want in this life? No, there *is* something I want…'

'Yes?'

'I would like to breathe.' He pulled his hands free and flung her cloak off him. He was about to get up, but when he saw her kneeling naked beside him he fell back and lay staring at her.

She slipped her arms around his chest and rested her head on his heart again. 'If you tell me to go away I will do it, if that is what you desire.'

He stroked her hair gently. 'What are you doing out here all alone?'

'I am not alone, but he refuses to be my lord, even though I know he loves me. He said that one day I would see another man, and know… it must be you, for when you rode by I felt the whole world was inside me… the hooves of your horse were the beating of my heart, the sun in my eyes was your hair, the sweat on your chest its warm light on my flesh, your black vest and blue eyes like the universe behind the daylight sky, and I felt my heart perch on your lips like a bird on a branch and everything joyously soared!'

He was silent.

'Does your wife feel the same way? I am certain she must.'

'Yes, but in the real world, life is not so simple.'

'Why?'

'Because, humans are complex beings…'

'You mean their roots have become tangled and they cannot simply be themselves?'

'Yes.' He laughed and suddenly pulled her down and kissed her, but then just as quickly he pushed her away.

A branch fell with a crack and was consumed as her mind fell blindly into his warmth. 'Tell me to go,' she pleaded, knowing that if he did not possess her wolves would stalk her later, scenting the pain of her unfulfilled desire, and all the food traps she had set would remain empty, like her body that had failed to catch his.

'Go,' he commanded softly, 'but first tell me your name.'

She sighed. 'I cannot unless you love me.'

He gazed at her breasts. 'How did you come to live out here?'

'It was my fate, and how it came to be was in the workings secretly from the day of my birth all the way back to the beginning of the earth.'

He smiled.

She frowned. 'But I do not understand why they gave you a wife before I entered your life.'

'Who is "they"?' he asked soberly.

'"They" is really we when we are higher beings.'

'What?'

'We plant our own lives as our hands do seeds. This body you have grown is only a single tree in your soul's infinite forest.'

'That makes sense. I like that.' He smiled again. 'Do you enjoy living out here?'

'Yes, but I am afraid that one day he will go steal another young girl from a village and leave me alone, so I have chosen you to be my lord.'

'Who is he?'

'He is my other half, yet he does not believe me when I tell him so, he thinks it is another for whom my heart is beating the night and day of this world... and perhaps he is right... I feel that it might be you, my lord...'

'Perhaps...' He pulled her down, rolling on top of her...

She stared, confused, into the darkness. *Where am I?* she thought. *Oh, yes, this is my room in the 21st century, whose colors he once played with....*

The phone rang.

*What an obnoxious little animal, crying out like that for attention! It must be Jim.* She got up quickly. *What the hell time is it?*

It *was* Jim's little figure standing on the receiver's black stage. 'How are you, baby?' he sounded especially serious.

'I'm okay, I was sleeping. What time is it? Where are you?'

'It's nine o'clock.'

'Nine o'clock? Aren't you coming to pick me up?'

'Were you having an interesting dream? I'm sorry if I interrupted anything.'

'I can't even remember what I was dreaming.' She felt a profound dismay at lying to him, yet the truth was impossible because she hardly knew what it was anymore. His idea that she still

desired Alex made her wonder if it wasn't true, yet all her heart and soul screamed her love for Jim, terrified at how the past was creeping jealous, paralyzing weeds into their growing love. She had started to wonder if he was using her old feeling for Alex to cover up his own guilt at wanting to loosen the reins of fidelity she had flung around him. 'Where are you, Jim?' she asked again, this time suspiciously.

'Visiting an old friend.' He glanced over his shoulder. 'Come into the screen and meet my wife. Don't worry, she'll understand, she has a nostalgic fancy for a blonde, too.'

No one appeared.

'Just kidding.'

'Fuck you!'

'No, don't switch me off, Elizabeth, we might as well face it now – you're still obsessed with Alex.'

'How can you say that? Why do you think that?' she asked desperately.

'You always have been, and, apparently, you always will be.'

'Jim, you're crazy, I love you!' She was crying.

'I think it's best if we separate for a while, Elizabeth. I'll pick you up tomorrow and you can pack whatever you need.'

She felt she was impossibly drowning in three feet of water; there was no reason for what was happening, they loved each other! 'Jim, you can't be serious.'

'The hell I'm not.'

'You bastard, you're using Alex as an excuse. You haven't changed a bit! You've never really loved me! I was just a novelty to you, a woman with brains, with a soul, for a change, but now that you've added my blue rose to your garden you're dying to go back to the picking, admit it!'

'I haven't been unfaithful to you,' he said quietly.

'Right!'

'Elizabeth, you *know* I love you.'

Her heart leapt with joy over the crack of despair in his voice.

'But you don't appreciate it.' His voice was terrifyingly calm again. 'I'm giving you the space and the time to realize it, that's all.'

'Why?' she gasped. 'Why are you doing this?'

'If I'm not around, there's a chance you'll start idealizing me, and maybe *I'll* become the main character in your dreams.' He vanished.

Elizabeth stared at where he had been, her eyes glassy as her life shattered around her. After timeless moments, she was unconsciously propelled into the kitchen by a gentle rumbling in her stomach which she knew meant her body was hungry. She clutched her stomach and doubled over sobbing. She had to live without him. Somehow, she had to survive the agony of his anger and the terrifying pain of living without him.

# Chapter Twenty-Four

It was raining heavily outside. She stood by her window at night, waiting, hoping, but the pure white curve of sidewalk remained a priest's collar around the darkness, for Jim never came. The storm was breaking every known record, which was a mysterious comfort to her, as if her broken heart still had power enough to drag the weather with it. As she wept, the wind howled sympathetically outside. Every hour she stalked her phone in a delirium of emotional and physical hunger, her body and soul having depended on him for so long she felt she might as well have lost her legs she spent so much time on her stomach sobbing. But he never called. After three days and nights of this – during which the sun never appeared as if her despair had shot it down point blank – her misery turned to fury.

*How dare he say that he loves me when he's killing me? To hell with him!* He was simply incapable of being faithful, and in a typical male fashion was blaming everything on her. Hell, so be it. If he wanted to thrust her back into Alex's arms, she'd fall willingly. Life didn't make any sense any more, so she might as well indulge her animal senses with Alex's enticingly forbidden meat...

She was a black cat crossing Alex's lawn through snow as high as her thin, freezing body. Jim had put her out, so she scratched and meowed helplessly at Alex's door, terrified that Linda would open it but irresistibly drawn to the luminous warmth emanating from beneath it. The cold caressed her painfully, like skeletal hands clutching her, and she was about to give up and let them take her when the door opened and she was lifted up into warm hands. She heard voices as she was set down gently, where she sprawled with joy in the golden grass of the rug, her stiff dark limbs melting languidly. Then everything happened like a dream – the full moon fell before her as a huge saucer of milk, and after that a blue plate descended like a wave full of glistening tuna, the smell of salt water and sun rushing through her and fully awakening her senses to the heaven above – his light-blue jacket a warm summer sky lit by his golden head. She collapsed in joy as the sun fell and the warm rays of his fingers restored her to life completely. She leapt onto his lap, curling up in its firm, deep warmth, at peace now and trying to stay awake to defend her territory, but easily falling asleep beneath his reassuring caresses...

She awoke, human, in her bedroom.

*It would be nice to be his cat, then Linda couldn't be jealous and he wouldn't have to feel guilty about petting me whenever he wanted to. Maybe someone will market such a formula. Keep your mistress a secret from your wife by turning her into a cat, comes in black, white or calico.* She chuckled miserably, gratefully falling asleep again...

It was mid summer and she lived in a cave above a beach which had remained isolated, for the cliffs were too sheer to climb and the waves too violent to safely capture in a tourist's brochure. Her body was limber as a spark covered in a dark, smoky flesh from the constant friction of salt water and sunshine. For hours she lay naked on the sand, the sun's intense penetration softened by the wind's caress. Whatever spirits ruled the ocean desired her – giant waves beat against her in a relentless, possessive rhythm, rising powerfully erect then collapsing in a roar of impotent fury between her thighs, tugging at her legs, longing to drown her in their embrace. At twilight their angry hissing turned to a cajoling whisper and they washed up gifts of oysters and clams, tasty silver fish of all sizes, ruby-red lobsters and moon-white crabs. She thanked them and carried her treasures up to her cave in a net she had made of seaweed, her nipples rounding and hardening like rosy pearls in the cool twilight breeze, her slender limbs easily navigating the rocks, the firm gravity of land and the sucking depth of the ocean in the curves of her waist and hips. She paused half way up the cliff to survey her domain. Sometimes as night fell she experienced a peace that had no other side it was so fine. She turned, finishing the ascent to her home, where Alex was sitting on a rock.

'I know this is a dream, but it's not very polite anyway,' he remarked, smiling.

'Please forgive me, sir.' She dropped her bundle and curtsied with an invisible skirt. 'Tomorrow night we shall meet in Victorian England and it will take you until morning to undress me.'

'Elizabeth...' He looked so serious she was afraid it would wake her up. 'What am I doing here?'

'I called you. Would you like some dinner? I have fresh lobsters.'

'No thanks, I ate before I went to bed... Jesus, this is strange, I realize I'm dreaming...'

'Isn't it great?' She abandoned the idea of food to begin undressing him. 'Here you don't have to feel guilty about anything.'

'Are you recording this?'

'Yes.' She pulled his shirt off.

'Then you could blackmail me, because only if I didn't realize I was sleeping with you would I technically be considered innocent.' He grinned, helping her remove his pants, but just as she slipped his penis into her mouth, he vanished. She looked behind her. Streaming impossible amounts of sea water, pearls webbed in his long hair, a red star fish covering his sex and seaweed clinging to his chest and thighs, stood Jim.

'What's the matter? Bored with all your devoted mermaids,

my king?' She spoke in the instant of turning, defensively stinging him with this jibe like a scorpion, before she saw that his face was as pale and sorrowful as a drowned man's. 'Jim!' she ran towards him, but she reached only a salty pool of tears on her pillow as she awoke.

The Dream Recorder clicked, satisfied, the jaws of an insect finishing its meal, a praying mantis devouring the butterfly of her imagination. The sound revolted her. She squirmed inside a cocoon of bed sheets, paralyzed with sorrow and guilt. He was right. He was right! She still wanted Alex.

# Chapter Twenty-Five

The next day Elizabeth was pleasantly surprised to get a call from Audrey. Mario's wife wanted to know if she felt like spending the day shopping, and Elizabeth was glad to accept the unexpected invitation. A day of mindless consumerism was just what she needed to get her mind off everything.

After she got home that evening, pleasantly worn out from walking through two malls and through Coral Moon's quaint antique shops, she entertained herself trying on the dresses she had bought, staring at herself in a full-length mirror, changing the colors of the room behind her to match each outfit. Going out shopping had recharged her. Nothing had changed on the outside, but inside she felt differently. *And that's all that counts in the end*, she thought.

Part of her new energy was that she felt infinitely superior to Alex. In a way, she despised his lifestyle – on the road for months, seeing his kid every few weeks, away from home when he was recording. 'Because he doesn't like distractions when he's working,' Linda had told her at the party.

'Distractions...' Elizabeth mumbled, stepping out of one dress and slipping into another 'I'm not a distraction, I'm an enhancement.' Her soul darkened with anger inside of her – a hot rush of feeling like the rash of a fever, Alex the sickness to which she was so pathetically and helplessly succumbing.

The door bell rang.

She glanced over her shoulder. 'Who could that be?' Then the hope surfaced its impossible, dragon-in-the-dream-moat head, and the fire of the possibility scalded her mind into a black, unconscious cinder for a few seconds, during which the bell rang again. She approached the door slowly, part of her terrified that whoever it was might leave if she didn't hurry, but she couldn't move any faster; gravity had suddenly thickened, and she felt as hot and flushed in her red-and-gold ankle-length dress as if she really was molten lava walking with the fatal slowness of its descent down a slope towards the door.

Alex was standing out on the landing holding a black duffel bag, and the sight was so impossible she just stared at him for a few seconds to make sure he was really there. He smiled his normal, carefree smile, but it was softer, dimmer, like the sun behind a cloud. And she knew *she* was this cloud – her imagination, all her dreams in which she used his image; borrowed some of his honest radiance to warm and illuminate her life. Her knees became weak and she thought, *Thank God, I do love him, I can't stand not loving him!* She looked down at the floor, stepping back away from the door, and to her relief, he entered her apartment. She had been irrationally afraid he was just going to stand there and confront her desire, kindly communicating to her its impossibility, and then leave forever.

She closed the door behind him. He set his bag down, and she searched desperately for something to say, but her mind felt like a garbage heap of meaningless statements with which she wouldn't even consider polluting the pure magic of his sudden presence.

'You look beautiful,' he said quietly. 'Are you going out?'

She wanted to dissolve in his arms, so she stared down at his black shoes and let her awareness cling to their steadily planted gravity. 'No, I was just trying on some things I bought today... Um, please sit down. Would you like something to drink?' she looked up at his face again and thought she would die because he wasn't smiling.

'No... I just got back into town.'

She walked over to the couch. 'Were you touring?' she asked, turning to face him again.

'No, recording... Why don't you keep trying on what you bought today and I'll tell you what I think.'

'All right... Well, you've seen this one.' She walked towards her bedroom, wishing she could think to say something entertaining, except there seemed to be no earthly reason to say anything. She felt like they were space walking, the flow of her dreams and his music the rarified oxygen they were breathing in these impossible moments outside of time and circumstance. She turned to close the bedroom door but he was behind her, following her into the room.

'Let me help you,' he said, and her awareness reeled at how close he was suddenly. She felt sucked into his black shirt and soft black leather jacket as into the void of space which instantly destroyed her ability to think; all she knew was the devastating need to merge with him.

He put his hands on her bare shoulders, turned her around, and unzipped her dress slowly, so that she could savor the gesture to the point of fear, because it was with her heart she was succumbing and he had given her no promise of an afterlife. He lifted her hair and unfastened the hook at the nape of her neck. Then his hands slipped beneath her arms to her breasts and pulled her dress down as they caressed her. She relaxed because there was no need to think now. The soft silk slipped down her thighs when he reached her sex. He gripped her mound with one hand while his other hand kneaded one of her breasts, and she knew what he was thinking then. He was angry, she felt it in the impatient way his fingers sought her clit and began arousing her with a cynical speed that seemed to say, 'You're no different from all the others.' She moaned and closed her eyes, her head falling back against his shoulder silently pleading with him. She thought that if he didn't kiss her soon she would die, and somehow he knew because he turned her around quickly. But they paused there, her arms around his neck, the dress twisted around her ankles, their lips almost touching as they stood eye-to-eye for a moment. Then in his kiss was flowingly, spelled out to her the knowledge his look had burned into her – he understood her love and he could appreciate its intensity. This acknowledgement was in the depth of his stare while the steadiness of his gaze told her it wouldn't change his life, that circumstances still separated them even as their limbs entwined.

# Chapter Twenty-Six

They lay in each others arms on her bed. 'You're quite a dreamer.' He smiled down at her and they made love again, swiftly, irresistibly, transforming the moment into a violent whirlpool of desire from which it was impossible to surface and think about anything. He loomed over her, beating his body against hers, his eyes closed in almost otherworldly concentration, his expression fascinating her to the point from which pleasure blossomed without end or effort as she watched him riding the ecstasy up past the scope of his consciousness. They came together again, kissing afterwards with the breathlessness of mouth-to-mouth resuscitation, recovering from the breathtaking depth of their shared pleasure.

They lay gaining strength, and she thought that if he got up to go now she would kill them both rather than let him. But she could tell he had no intention of moving, and no strength to do so for that matter. His face was buried between her neck and shoulder, the soft harbor where he recovered himself after pumping all his energy into her. She caressed him gently, thinking that she wanted to please him until he was unconscious from the intensity of the fulfillment. The walls of her room glowed red-and-gold like suspended flames around them, their bodies like two slender pieces of wood rubbing together producing them. She wanted to ask him how long he could stay, but was terrified to bring it up. He drew back and she stared into his eyes for a long time, except there was no such thing then, so it could very well have gone on forever without her ever thinking about anything except him. He caressed her idly and she became self-conscious, wondering what images she could offer him now that she had him, and she realized there could be no greater magic than simply lying in his arms. But this filled her with despair, because Linda had nine years head start there.

She sat on top of him, staring down into his eyes and caressing his chest wondering what she could do for him that no one else could besides adore him unconditionally, never trying to pressure him into anything, giving him total freedom, which was exactly what her woman's nature did not want to do. But she would, she would be like his music, there when he wanted her, when his touch made her come alive again, perfectly silent when he did not feel her, even if it meant weeks or months without seeing him. The only thing she could do was send him her dreams, enveloping him in the magical atmosphere of her love.

He played with her breasts, his spent erection remaining contemplatively soft beneath her, and her soul rested in his tender expression.

Thunder rumbled outside.

'Are you hungry?' she asked him, as if the sound had come from his stomach, and after a second they laughed, because the slip revealed what god-like proportions he possessed in her heart.

'As a matter of fact, I am. What've you got?'

But she stopped smiling as she remembered what Jim had said, that love controls the elements, because she distinctly felt at that moment that their passion was affecting the weather. She knew it was so, and the thought of where they could go from there stabbed her with such an acute sense of excitement that she fell back down beside him. She wanted to tell him what she had just thought, but she bit her lip to stop herself from suggesting that together they could share experiences he and Linda never could. Yet she had gotten the distinct impression that their physical embrace was only the seed of a more powerful and captivating union involving the combined energy of their souls.

'Alex…' She wanted him to reassure her that he was going to stay all night. 'What would you like?' she said instead.

'Well, let's see what you've got.'

They got out of bed, but then stood kissing for a while beside it before finally venturing into the kitchen. It was wondrous for Elizabeth to see him standing naked beneath the bright light in front of the open refrigerator studying the colorful interior. She leaned against him, not at all hungry for food, just for him.

'Hmm, let's see…' He smiled, deliberately taking his time, knowing what was on her mind as her hand moved possessively down his naked body. 'How about if we start with a little milk since we're standing here like the day we were born?' He pulled out the half gallon carton. 'Here, baby…' He held it up to her lips and she swallowed what she could, but most of it ran down her chin and onto her breasts. She cried out because the milk was cold, and he put the carton back quickly to lick her, his warm tongue a delicious contrast. 'I have an idea,' he said, and she liked it already because of his tone. 'Why don't you go lie on the table…'

He removed the pimentos from two large olives and stuffed them with her nipples before placing a juicy grape in her navel. Then he wrapped a slice of ham around her neck and lay a square of butter on her lips so she couldn't laugh or talk only moan when she felt him insert something cold and hard into her pussy. He gripped her thighs, biting into whatever he had filled her with, and she realized it was a drumstick. The hard bone moved against her as he consumed the tender meat around it, and since it was emerging from her she felt as if he was really eating her. The mental excitement of this, combined with the pressure of the bone against her clitoris and the possessive grip of his hands on her thighs, gave her intense pleasure.

The butter was melting on her lips when he finally pulled the bone out. He got on the table with her then, bent over her and devoured her nipples, chewing on the olives as he licked her mouth; sucking on each butter-stained lip before he began feasting on her neck, so that when he finished she had the exquisite feeling of having been literally consumed by him. He fell against her then, crushing the grape in her navel, and its sweet juice felt like her own as he penetrated her.

\* \* \*

They showered together and Elizabeth didn't recognize him when his hair got wet and darkened, matting against his forehead and falling into his eyes. She pushed it away gently and stared at the face of a stranger there with her in the pure space of her bathroom, his lips the horizon separating his soul from hers. Yet when they touched, dimensions ceased to exist and she experienced the wholeness of the universe in his kiss.

They set about the task of soaping each other up and gave into every pleasurable distraction. He took an impossible amount of time on her breasts, and as he sucked on her slick hard nipples she wondered at how much men enjoy re-enacting their infancy. There was no milk for him there now just her soft cries of pleasure, and this seemed to be what his feeling was being nourished with.

They towelled each other dry and she kept looking from him to their ghostly forms in the misted shower door, spellbound by his naked flesh which was nevertheless a mysterious layer of clothing over the eternal energy of his spirit. She embraced him, and he let her just hold him for a while.

'Come on,' he whispered, and they stepped back out into the bedroom. He lay on his back on the bed, looking up at her as she knelt beside him, trembling with excitement and terror at what she wanted to do now, what she had done for Jim so many times so casually. But now she was so full of awe at the prospect that her cheek fell against his firm stomach. She felt weak from the quivering intensity of the suspense like an arrow in her heart that put her completely at his mercy. She caressed his soft, warm penis delicately, but was reassured by its resilience that she wouldn't hurt him if she tightened her possessive grip and licked it, full of wonder at how similar to Jim's cock it was in size and width and yet how absolutely different, possessed of its own unique personality. He wasn't as easily fulfilled by oral sex as Jim was either, and this fascinated and excited her, yet also frightened her so much that tears welled up in her eyes, slipping down her cheeks and bathing his erection in the salty depths of her feelings for him. But her long, dark hair hid her face so that he couldn't see that she was crying.

The experience of going down on him exhausted her, but when she tasted his cum and felt it flowing down her throat, the pleasure of swallowing his essence made all her efforts worthwhile. She pushed her hair away from her face, peeling strands sticky with his sperm from her lips, and looked at him. His eyes were closed, his mouth slightly parted, and his expression devastated her beyond any rational power to define why and enable her to control her reaction. She curled up on the bed with her back to him and wept silently, part of her ashamed that he should see her, another part of her wanting for him to help her understand and deal with it.

'Elizabeth?' he touched her arm, but she kept her face hidden beneath her hair.

'I love you,' she confessed.

He turned her around gently and held her against him, but he didn't say anything, and to her dismay she began to fall asleep in the deep comfort of his arms.

# Chapter Twenty-Seven

She woke and thought her room was on fire, the red and gold flames of the walls licking up into her consciousness reflecting unusual warmth all around her. Then she realized with a sweet, sinking joy that the warmth was emanating from Alex's sleeping body beside hers. She took a slow, shuddering breath of relief that he wasn't gone, but then remembered, like the point of an icicle touching her heart, that soon it would be morning. She moaned in agony and he stirred. She felt guilty because she didn't want to disturb him, but she also couldn't endure wasting a single, precious instant with him. She caressed the nape of his neck, and the softness of his hair, combined with the full weight of his arm, almost hypnotized her back into sleep. But then he stirred abruptly and desire roused her completely. He had surfaced a little from the depths of sleep although he was still breathing deeply, and she half urged, half pulled him on top of her, spreading her legs. And the pleasure of his unconscious weight against her aroused her in the strangest way, as if the length of his body replaced the line dividing the left and right sides of her brain and she was perfectly conscious even as she became pure feeling. He began moving against her with a helpless urgency, still half asleep and dreaming he was inside her.

'Alex!' she whispered, reaching down with one hand to

caressing his stiffening cock gently but purposefully. He stopped breathing heavily and raised his head, awake. He felt her hand and promptly lifted her legs around him, caressing the backs of one of her thighs urgently. She touched her hot, hungry opening with his head, making them become acquainted and driving herself wild, because in the intimate languor of sleep they knew each other so well already that prolonging the separation was nothing but torture. He kissed her with a breathless passion, raising his body like a horse bucking the gentle passage of her hands off him as he thrust his erection deep and hard into her pussy. Her innermost flesh gripped his possessively, milking him passionately. She could feel his eyes on her in the dark, and as she stared, she saw them shining above her like distant stars.

\* \* \*

Elizabeth woke first again and it made her sick to see the daylight swelling behind her window shade as if already self-satisfied and bloated with his being that it would soon take him away from her, dispersing him into circumstances and the warmth of other peoples' affections, whereas right now he was all hers, just himself, in her arms.

*I wish he had left in the dark again*, she thought, and got up slowly and silently to use the bathroom and to try and prepare herself for what was coming. She splashed cold water on her face, hoping it would snap her into a more realistic state, but it was no use. She brushed her hair and its soft fullness only enhanced her sensation of still floating at the heart of the universe in his kiss. She put on black eyeliner to enhance the sad mystery of her eyes, so that he would know how she felt without her having to say anything. She really felt incapable of saying a word, as if it would be regressing to meaningless baby sounds and only silence was mature communication. She slipped on her white house dress, braced herself, and walked back out into the bedroom.

He was lying on her bed as she had first seen him, with his hands under his head, staring at her blank viewing screen, only he was already naked. He smiled at her when she emerged, and she felt she would die because of how sweet and young he looked, his blonde hair fallen over his forehead and into his eyes. She knelt on the edge of the bed to brush it away, irresistibly smiling back at him, and he pulled her down into his arms so they could make love again.

\* \* \*

They lay in each other's arms, the morning growing older, yet he still wasn't gone, and she began to wonder. She almost wished he would leave so she could get the initial agony over with and settle into a comfortable despair, half of her already involved in it and tainting the joy she was taking in his continued presence.

'I'm supposedly out of town again for a few days,' he said abruptly, and she knew what Lazarus had felt when the tomb door rolled off his shoulders and the world opened up to him again. Her breathing slowed almost to the point of ceasing, strangely suspended between life and death as she waited for him to continue.

'Your dreams have affected my playing, Elizabeth, they've reminded me of what a beautiful, sensual instrument the guitar is and of how much I really love it.'

She kept her eyes cast down, gazing at his chest, but she felt it was time for her to speak. 'I'm here for you.'

'You know what a fortune teller told me?' he asked.

'What?' she laughed, amused that anyone who was already so fortunate should be told his fortune.

'She said, "One day you will meet a woman who possesses the same intensity and creative spirit as your music, and you won't be able to leave her behind for weeks at a time because she *is* your music, her body is your instrument, and the vast darkness of the concert hall is the unlimited magic of the universe". That's what she said.'

'You fucking liar!' she laughed, looking up into his eyes, but he began kissing her so she never found out if it was true or not. Then it occurred to her, with the same slight shock she experienced whenever he penetrated her, that if he had just said it himself it was even more true because the statement came from his own understanding. Her body went limp in his arms and for a terrified moment she was sure she was asleep and dreaming. But no, his hands were real, almost too real, suddenly, gripping the back of her neck and her thigh possessively while his tongue wandered lazily in her mouth, because she was his and he could do as he pleased with her.

# Chapter Twenty-Eight

'Art is fifth dimensional training.'

Alex laughed, 'Is that so?' He pulled her to him.

'Yes, I know it is.' She rested her head on his chest and closed her eyes.

'You know a lot,' he remarked quietly.

'I only know as much as you make me feel.'

'Is that so?' he repeated, and she noticed how often he used that expression, as if it was a force-field deflecting her statement to give him time to ponder it. She could tell part of him was amazed she was always spontaneously saying things like that, but that another part of him understood her perfectly. It was their first afternoon together and they had only gotten out of bed to have some brunch. 'We're going to forget how to walk,' he had said.

'Well, then let's journey into the living room.' She jumped out of bed and searched her dresser.

'What are you looking for?' He came up behind her and put his hands distractingly on her hips, looking over her shoulder.

She quickly pulled out a long, wide scarf before she could forget what she was doing. 'Here, I want you to wear this.' She turned to face him and he closed the drawer with the weight of their bodies. 'Alex, stop, we're just going to end up on the bed again.'

'Okay.' He stepped back and looked at what she was holding. 'Why the hell do you want me to wear that?'

'Because, it will please me to look at you in it.' It was a white scarf decorated with a pattern of lines and triangles. She wrapped it around his hips like a loincloth. 'This is all men used to wear in ancient times.' She tied it into a knot on the side. 'Besides, while you're in my apartment, you're in a temple.'

'Then I get to pick what you're going to wear.' He glanced at her jewel box. 'Nothing but jewels.' He picked it up. 'Now into the living room with you, wench!'

They reclined across her Oriental rug, but then she got up again to disconnect her phone, relieved no one had called before it occurred to her to do so, because any interruption of his presence would have been unendurable. She pulled up the blinds and he was suddenly bathed in a ray of light. She gazed at him in pure awe as he studied the contents of her jewel box. He lifted item after item and her faux gems flashed in the sunlight like priceless treasures. He appeared fascinated by their sparkle and the warm depth of the colors and seemed to have forgotten her, but then he yelled, 'Where the hell are you?!' and she smiled and lay down beside him.

'These are awesome,' he said, referring to her earrings. He held up a large silver pair – a star with a diamond in its center and a crescent beneath it with little hearts and crosses dangling from it. 'Put these on... no, wait...' He kept catching sight of other pieces that fascinated him. He fingered her silver fish, and she smiled at his expression when he realized they were supple as the real thing, the fins flapping delicately back and forth with her motion. 'How the hell am I supposed to decide?' he mumbled, and she kept smiling dreamily, because colors and forms made such perfect sense in his hands. 'Wear these.' He finally stuck with his first choice.

'These are my priestess earrings.' She put them on as he watched her. They were large but light and she knew the crescent shone like the real thing inside the darkness of her hair. 'The moon is a fingertip that points to a different person for everyone, and for me it points to you,' she said, waiting for another, 'Is that so?' from him, but it didn't come, he just stared at her face for a moment then resumed his exploration of her treasures.

*If I think about what's happening, I won't believe it*, she thought as he dressed her with jewels – a crystal necklace glimmering the spectrum against her flesh; two other necklaces that hung down past her navel made of luminous green and gold beads; a host of bracelets, thin silver ones that coiled around her wrists like serpents, and wide beaten gold ones that clung to her upper arms; and finally an ankle bracelet that jingled musically when she shook her leg before him, laughing. 'I feel like a jewelry mannequin,' she protested.

'I forgot about rings.' He slipped one onto each of her fingers without bothering to select them, sitting cross-legged before her. He studied her and she untied his makeshift loincloth to caress his penis so he could watch gems flashing and glowing around it in the sunlight. She licked his stiffening cock, the stars and crescents dangling against his growing erection as if magically protecting it while it gradually rose the way waves do beneath the moon's magnetic pull. She looked up at his face, feeling his cock hardening as his eyes dimmed, his awareness passing from one head to another, one conceptual and the other experiential, his soul the mysterious marvel of the two combined.

'Come here,' he whispered, grasping her wrists and pulling her arms up around his neck as she straddled him. His penis found her hole and slid inside her easily, familiarly. It happened too suddenly and smoothly for her; she hadn't been able to prepare for the wonder of union with him. She buried her face in his neck, avoiding his eyes. 'Look at me, Elizabeth,' he murmured, holding her motionless against him, his cock buried deep in her belly.

She obeyed him, and green and golden beads beat gently against her womb as he gripped her hips and slid her pussy slowly up and down his hard-on, the firm intimacy of his stare merging with the stiffness of his cock in such a way that his expression became her pleasure as he slowly stroked himself with her slick, tight hole. She kissed him to cool the intensity of his stare, not knowing what he was thinking making it hurt; the penetration of his eyes arousing a pained, virginal excitement in her soul so that she knew he was the first man she had ever really loved. When she and Jim had looked at each other, it had provided an arousing challenge, but Alex's eyes filled her with the profound peace of walking beside the ocean beneath the sky, the waves breaking the years of her life and of the earth without changing how she felt about him for as long as they lived. And when the world ended it would only be him closing his eyes in sleep to dream another one that the force of her love would create for him. Jim had intellectually humored her idea of being Isis, but her love for Alex made her literally feel a divine power inside of her.

'What are you thinking?' he asked, abruptly.

'Nothing,' she said, and then laughed softly, because it was more like everything, the entire universe, but now he was asking for a sip and she couldn't find the words, like a cup, to give it to him. He caressed her intently, but the physical joy was only the byproduct of a much deeper one.

Afterwards they held each other for a moment before she moved off his lap. He fell onto his back and she reclined on her side beside him gazing down the length of his body. He lay staring up at the ceiling, and for some reason this made her realize how exhausted she was. She rolled onto her back, following his example, and it was soothing to stare at the straight lines and angles of the room enjoying the settled confinement that had dissolved in their union. Especially when he slipped his hand into hers and they lay staring up together.

Finally, he sat up. 'You know, I never did see your paintings.' He pushed himself to his feet and walked over to the wall where they hung.

'I'll fix us some dinner while you do.' She picked up the scarf-loincloth and lovingly wrapped it around him again before removing all her jewelry except for the earrings. Then she went into the kitchen and took a great, simple pleasure in the colors and textures and smells of the food and the herbs she used to season it.

He strolled in after a while and came up behind her, keeping his hands to himself because he had a vested interest in what she was doing, but looking over her shoulder curiously and hopelessly distracting her. 'I love your paintings,' he said, and she gave up, turning around to hug him passionately.

\* \* \*

They were eating and she was thinking, *This is glorious, but how am I going to deal with it when he's gone? It's going to be hell. But no, I can look forward to him coming again. Or can I? What is he thinking? How does he feel? I don't even really know, do I?*

She lost her appetite. She put her fork down and concentrated on her wine, returning his smile as he devoured his food with the single-minded pleasure of a hungry little boy.

*I know he loves Linda, so he can't love me. ..He probably just likes me a lot and is under the spell of my dreams, responding to my love like a child to candy... He's going for a ride on it like a kid in Magic Land... But that's not fair, he's not a child... although he is, he's so sweet... yet he understands what I say, he knows it's all true... but you can only have one soul mate, so he either loves me or Linda.*

She couldn't even swallow her wine now. He looked at her and she smiled softly, shaking her head, indicating that she wasn't hungry. They were in the kitchen and the plain, utilitarian surroundings only heightened the intense wonder of his presence. He finished eating and she thought, *Help!*

\* \* \*

'You can tell what a person is like just by the way he walks,' she said conversationally watching Alex walk from the bathroom back to her bed later that evening.

'Can you really?' He sat on the edge of the mattress and smiled down at her.

'Yes, you can. When I saw a DVD of one of your concerts, the way you walked enthralled me.'

'Oh, really?'

'Yes. You walked from the dressing room out onto the stage with such self-confident gravity. I can't describe it, but most people just don't walk like that. Once I passed some men on the street and they said, "What do you call that, the moon walk, sweet heart"? They got the metaphysics of my personality down just by my walk.'

He laughed. 'Elizabeth, you're unreal!'

'Oh, I am, am I?' She gripped his cock with one hand and the back of his neck with the other, pulling his head down to kiss him. 'How unreal do I feel now?' she asked against his mouth, and he bit her lip, caressing her as she caressed him. But then abruptly he flung her hands away, pushed her over onto her stomach and knelt on the bed between her legs. He clutched her hips, pulled them up against him, and penetrated her from behind with an impatient, selfish force. He growled at the encumbrance of hair, and she reached up and flung it forward so he could bite her neck as he thrust himself deep into her yielding pussy. Then she fell onto her stomach and lay utterly still beneath his violent, ramming strokes because her passivity seemed to please him.

'You're wondering if I love you, aren't you, Elizabeth?' he whispered into her hair. 'I just know I had to be with you...'

'But you don't know how you'll feel a few days from now,' she said coolly.

'No,' he admitted, jamming his erection so deep inside her she cried out.

'I'm sorry!' she gasped, feeling she had no right to put him in this position. Yet she couldn't argue with her soul's need for love.

He pulled out of her, rolled her over onto her back, and stared down into her eyes. 'Don't be sorry.'

She sighed. 'Whatever you say.'

'So if I tell you I'll only be able to see you every now and then, it's all right with you?' he asked gently and she couldn't read his expression. She wanted to say, 'Yes!' right away, because a part of her was trembling with fear at the thought of not seeing him at all, but another part of her clamped down like an oyster over the long-suffered pearl of her soul, whose value was far too great to accept such a meager offer.

*Better nothing,* she thought, *than just starting all over with him every time, we'll never get anywhere like that.*

'Yes,' she said.

'You're lying.' He smiled.

She nodded, irresistibly returning his smile because it always managed to wash all her concerns away like a ray of sunlight entering a shadow-filled room. Then he started moving inside of her again and she forgot everything, slipping her arms around him and reaching up to kiss him. But he rose up on his arms, sliding in and out of her with the uncertain air of not knowing whether he wanted to stay or leave and destroying her pleasure, which was mysteriously delicate in proportion to its intensity. Then he beat against her as if he had made his

decision and was fighting her off, eliminating her from his system with a swift, mechanical fucking and climax that would leave their souls cold and alienate them from each other.

'No!' she whimpered, closing her eyes.

'I love you!' he said angrily, thrusting the words into her as he came.

# Chapter Twenty-Nine

They were devouring a dish-full of fruit on her carpet at midnight. She grabbed his apple and rested her head in his lap, looking up at him. 'Here, Adam.'

He bit into it. 'Oh, my God, Elizabeth, you're naked!'

'That's right, we're out of the garden, honey.'

He played with her breasts. 'I don't know about that...'

'Alex, lets be serious,' she said suddenly.

'Okay.' He grinned down at her.

'I know how busy you are and that there are people that you love I can never take you away from... I just want to know I can have you all to myself like this some times...'

'I thought you wanted me all the time.'

'I do.'

'You're contradicting yourself, then.'

'No... that would be the ideal thing, but...'

'Well, if you're my music, Elizabeth, you'll have to go on tour with me... which means you'll be on the road away from your Dream Recorder for weeks at a time. Could you handle that?'

'Are you kidding? I'd be *living* in a dream.'

'It's no dream,' he warned firmly. 'It gets pretty exhausting after a while, there's really nothing glamorous about it...'

'Oh, to hell with glamour! I'll have both you and your music;

I'll be in Nirvana. I'll live inside you, dancing until I drop dead every night, and wake up in your arms in the morning. Bliss, absolute bliss. I don't care if I have to eat cat food in between.'

'It's not *that* bad!'

'Just think of me as your mascot... my soul belongs to your music like a cat.'

'Elizabeth, why are you always saying things like that? How do they apply to real life?'

The abrupt seriousness of his tone took her by surprise and clearly indicated to her that he was fighting a battle inside himself. Half of him related to the things she said, the other half was firmly planted in the literalness of reality. She could see this reflected in his life, the power and mystery of his music rooted in a realistically disciplined life-style. But his soul flowed freely with it like a tree in the wind, and this was the source of his strength, his still blossoming creativity – the knowledge that his music was his spirit and that was where his freedom lay ultimately and forever. He stared into her eyes waiting for a response to a question he did not really feel had an answer, she could tell by the kind sternness of his expression. She smiled. 'It will never be true on a visible level,' she told him. 'I mean, I'll never look like a cat, and your music will never coalesce into a big hand and caress me, but on an invisible level the analogy is very real. If you believe in the metaphysics of life, that's what happens – my soul responds to your music with the same instinctive, one-hundred percent sensuality and vital joy as a cat to its owner. The only difference is I give magic back with the things I say... with the dream realms my arms open up out of love for you.'

He smiled down at her. 'But these dream realms only exist on a DVD.'

'In this space, in the fifth dimension they'll be real.'

'What's the fifth dimension?'

'The fifth dimension is where you will be when you open the door of the grave.'

'What if I'm cremated?'

'Then you'll turn into a cloud and your feeling will rain down and grow any world it pleases.' She smiled up at him triumphantly.

'I see. Do you really believe all this, Elizabeth?'

'Yes, and if you want to know how it relates to life, when you're dead your inner space is the outer world, your creativity its fluidity, your heart its sun. The after-death experience used to be a mass affair in the ancient world, and in the early days of Christianity, but death can be a terrible experience now because organized religions have lost their power and an inner life, an imagination, is considered a superfluous luxury, an essentially powerless entertainment, so that the fifth dimension, for a great majority of souls, is a featureless darkness.. a vast Hollywood dumpster crawling with phantasmagorical vermin!'

'Elizabeth!'

They laughed and he cupped her face in his hands, gently tracing her cheeks and lips with his thumbs, their slow caressing revealing that his reason was falling under her spell.

'There you're divided from people by inner, not outer, space,' she went on, waxing eloquent beneath his reverent caress. 'Those with whom your soul has affinity can come into your experience, because visibility is determined by affection. If those you loved on earth don't believe in the immortality of the soul, you won't be able to see them, to feel their presence, so you can imagine what pain a lot of souls who have left loved ones behind experience nowadays.

Because it's the heart that illuminates the afterworld, the earth's sun is only a symbol of the eternal, luminous force at the heart of every individual spirit. And if we want to be reborn...'

'What determines that?'

'Well... if you want to know how to play the guitar you practice, wanting to get better and better until you can play whatever you desire, and that's the nature of mortality and rebirth, to develop our creative skill...'

'But we won't have bodies…'

'We won't have corporeal bodies, but our images will remain in a form a thousand times more sensual like moving pictures made of light, only in the fifth dimension you'll be inside the hot flow of the image and feel everything. You'll still have a form, it just won't be this limited, solid and pathetically fragile one.'

He bent down and kissed her, squeezing her nipples to feel her tongue shudder in response and circle his wildly as he rubbed her stiff peaks slowly between his thumb and forefinger.

He drew back. 'Where were you?'

'I don't know…' Her eyes remained closed as he continued playing with her breasts.

'Go on,' he said as she whispered, 'Don't stop!'

# Chapter Thirty

'No,' she whispered, not letting go of him.
'Soon, Elizabeth, soon,' he assured her softly.
'No.' She let her arms slip from around his neck feeling as though her soul was land-sliding down from heavenly heights to the plain, crowded world again; into a city swarming with human beings that meant nothing to her. And now he was going out amongst them, leaving their personal Nirvana. She could not understand; the thought of Linda no longer aroused the black hopelessness that had served as an inkwell to spell out life's limitations and her own guilt. She no longer believed in either one. A few days in his arms had transformed her perception of the world. Her senses and emotions burned in a way that illuminated everything. She now saw Linda as being in the wrong because she wanted only to possess him, not to elevate him. All Linda wanted was a comfortable nest with him in these dimensions, while Elizabeth desired to fly off with him into endless creative fantasies.

But he was still leaving, and she supposed she should understand, but it only made her feel strange, as though he had an illness of which he was refusing to cure himself. She stared down at the floor as they stood silently beside the front door.

'Elizabeth, you knew this moment would come.' There was no hesitation in his voice and no strain of sympathy, which strangely enough made her feel hopeful. That he wasn't sorry for her was an indication of how deeply he felt for her.

'Yes, I knew, just like I know I'm going to die, but I still don't believe it, I still want eternity with you.'

He averted his eyes. 'You're not going to die.'

'No, my heart is as safe as a bird in the cage of my ribs... but if you don't love me I'll never fly high again inside ...the days will just go by one after the other like birdseed...'

'Elizabeth, stop.' He looked into her eyes, his willpower penetrating her desire and dissolving her soul helplessly around its arousing firmness.

'I'm sorry.' She lowered her head again. 'It's just that I adore you.' She bit her lip, tears of unwanted devotion welling up into her eyes, and thought, *Tears are what holy water is made of. Dip your fingers in them, Alex, and make the sign of the cross, because I worship you.*

'Oh, Jesus!' He pulled her roughly to him and she wrapped her arms around his body, her mind going blank against his heart. There was no past, no future, and thus no pain, there was only him.

'I'll come by Sunday night,' he promised. It was Monday morning.

'No.' She doesn't know how she did it, but she pulled away from him and walked towards her paintings as if to draw strength from their magical depiction of reality in these painfully real moments. 'We shouldn't see each other again because it'll just kill me.' There, it was out, she had said it, now she could relax. Until he put his hands on her shoulders, then it was as if the sky fell on her when he turned her around to face him and she was forced to look up into his eyes.

'Do you really mean that?' His mouth was firm, stretching her soul over it like a torture rack.

'Yes!' She sounded angry because she wanted him to fuck her again and had to fight the desire because it was so rooted in the moment, her body unconcerned with the eternity of love. It was saying, 'Accept the clouds and the sunshine, take him when he comes, relax and don't think about him when he's gone.'

'Do you really?' he asked again quietly, pulling her to him by the hips as he held her eyes.

'No...' She barely heard her own voice she was so weak from the terrible need to feel him inside her again.

He smiled. 'Elizabeth, you're always contradicting yourself.'

'Oh, God, I hate you,' she breathed, quickly unbuttoning the top half of his shirt and slipping her hands beneath it, nourishing herself with the firm warmth of his chest. But then she saw his duffel bag sitting by the front door. She stepped away from him and buttoned his shirt back up. 'Get out of here.' She tried to sound casual, avoiding his stare. 'I'll stop behaving like quicksand and let you go.' But something happened when their eyes met again, like a short circuit in which she literally felt the sparks of his emotions burning into her soul.

'Elizabeth!' He pulled her to him and it was a volcanic eruption of love for him that flowed out of the throbbing of her heart, an earthquake-like trembling of her limbs as he caressed her and pushed her back against the wall, kissing her so furiously that thoughts tumbled like rubble past the window of her consciousness and she was free, a pure force, as he lifted her leg and caressed her thigh, holding it up around him. She tightened her arms around his neck, her body pressed against the wall and her raised leg at one with the space of the room holding him. She had no intention of letting him go, he would live inside her forever, going wherever he pleased but always coming back to her. They somehow managed to separate to pull down her panties and open his pants, moaning at how horribly long it seemed to take. Her soul seemed unable to breathe outside his kiss like a mermaid exiled from the warm flow of the ocean where she rode joyously on the currents of his feelings, perfectly free of the gravity of thoughts except for the eternal concern of pleasing him.

He took her swiftly and violently, and after the devastation of the orgasm he shook his head as if returning to consciousness after an accident, disoriented, pulling away from her abruptly as if afraid that part of him was fatally wounded and it was all her fault. At the same time she savored holding onto his heart a moment longer, until his head cleared and she felt his willpower pull it out of her hands again.

'I have to go, Elizabeth.' He avoided her eyes, closing his pants and turning away from her.

She didn't say anything as she smoothed down her short red dress, her blue panties crumpled at her feet.

He walked over to the door and picked up his bag, only then turning to face her again.

'Have a good life, I never want to see you again,' she said, and knew he couldn't believe it by the way he stood there almost supernaturally motionless, as if trying to catch the echo of her words and define what she had really said. 'What are you still doing here?' she sobbed, collapsing onto her couch and burying her face in her hands, furiously determined to hold back the tears until she heard the door close behind him. But the sound didn't come, so she looked up again to postpone the breaking point inside, and was confronted with the vision of him kneeling before her, gripping her wrists gently and burying his face in her hands.

'I didn't know it was going to be like this, Elizabeth.' He kissed her palms.

'Oh, Alex, I worship you, I'm sorry.' She caressed his hair, soothing herself with its straight, simple softness.

'But it's only like this in the beginning...'

'Is it?' She understood what he was saying, that if they saw each other all the time the intensity of their love would dim, become more realistic; based on a fond familiarity and emotional synchronicity, essentially a friendship with polarity, like his marriage with Linda. He was saying that only beginnings or rare meetings possessed this all-consuming quality.

'Yes.' He kissed her palms again as if apologizing to her love and life lines for having become a part of them.

'That's not true, Alex, I've never felt this way about anyone and I never will again.' She told him this despite how dramatic it sounded, because she knew it was true beyond a shadow of a doubt now.

'Don't think that, Elizabeth,' he said firmly, but they were wading softly in each other's eyes. He rose, pulling her up with him, and pressed her hands reassuringly as he spoke. 'I don't know what's going to happen yet, I just need to know that you'll be expecting me on Sunday…'

She lowered her head. 'Of course.'

# Chapter Thirty-One

The doorbell rang. She was lying on her couch listening to Alex's music and feeling every note of his guitar like a penetration. This had been her position for the last few days, altered only to perform the necessary, mundane actions of physical existence. Her body was exhausted, but her soul seemed only to have been warmed up. Her eyes closed, she was quite literally flowing on the waves of the music, every little note of his guitar striking her veins, her body having become the instrument of his self-expression. It was a state of muscular exhaustion yet perpetual exaltation, and she felt she was getting a brief, spoon-like taste of what it was like in the fifth dimension when she could throw off her tired flesh and embody this love she felt for him.

She looked at the door without rising because she knew with a hauntingly infallible certainty that it wasn't Alex. He had said Sunday night and it was only Thursday morning. The bell rang again twice, insistently, and she got up finally as the last notes of a song filled the room, a vibration of sound slowly fading out like the shock waves of pleasure after orgasm.

'Coming!' She turned off the disk player, smoothed out her royal-blue slip, and opened the door.

Jim was standing before her wearing his perennial black leather pants and a loose white cotton shirt open half way down his chest. He stared at her, his small eyes as sharp as fangs flashing into her soul with resentment and jealous curiosity.

'Hello, Jim,' she said. 'Won't you come in?' She smiled because her monotone rhyme gave a powerlessly silly air to his dramatic confrontation.

'What's the big idea taking the phone off the hook?' He shoved her aside. 'What's been going on here?' He walked right over to the bedroom and looked inside it, and after a subliminal hesitation he disappeared and Elizabeth knew he was checking the bathroom.

She closed the front door unwillingly and leaned against it, completely amazed by his behavior and trying to think. This intrusion was too sudden and unexpected for her to deal with in her condition. He re-appeared in the bedroom door, significantly framed by it, and she straightened, her mind still unfocused, but vitally on guard. 'What do you want, Jim?' she asked, and felt the acid indifference of her voice hit the cauldron of his emotions with a fatal explosion.

'You bitch!' he whispered.

*His light is dim*, she thought. *How could I have ever believed he was so intense?* 'Jim, calm down,' she demanded, unable to understand his sudden jealousy, and starting to worry about his behavior.

'Elizabeth, come here, baby,' he pleaded, and she felt as though he hit her behind the knees. 'I need you, Elizabeth. I miss you so much. Please come here...' It was the soft, hypnotic voice she remembered, but even more devastating because of its utterly helpless quality.

'Oh, Jim!' She closed her eyes, her head falling back against the door. She felt as though he had just struck her viciously calculated blows.

'Oh, God, baby, I've missed you!' She seemed to hear his voice drawing nearer but couldn't bring herself to look at him. 'I need you, Elizabeth...' Then she felt him and she opened her eyes when his hands closed over her breasts, kneading them as if they were her mind and he could convince her like this. She flung them off passionately, slipping away from him lithely, but there was nowhere to go, every part of the room opening up to her vision like a trap – the deep, blood-red rug, the soft black couch, the distant white bed floating inside the blue glow of the bedroom – so she turned and faced him again.

He gripped her shoulders, the focused penetration of his stare like the point of a sword disarming her with the intensity of his willpower. 'You're still mine, Elizabeth…' His hands slipped down her arms with the weight of this statement, his caress telling her it was quite a pleasant fact if she would only let herself feel it as such. And meanwhile his face was hypnotizing her with the memory of all the climaxes in which she had seen it rising over her like this, the curving softness of his lips the beds they had lain in, the haunting depth of his eyes all the nights in which they had made love. But even as she was lost in the experience, she knew his face was affecting her only as a deep cushion of memory, but that she felt nothing for him now. What she felt was the haunting twilight glow of all their burning unions, and after it was gone she saw him clearly and stepped back, slipping her hands out of his.

'It won't work, Jim,' she said, and the angry twist of his lips seemed to wring him out of her soul completely.

'You certainly don't seem too sex-starved,' he observed.

She took another step back, filled with distaste.

He smiled. 'I get it, Alex has been here, that's why you took the phone off the hook.'

'No.' For the first time since his arrival she was trembling with terror, the thought that he should in any way interfere with what was happening just too horrible to fathom. 'I haven't seen him since the party,' she lied calmly.

'Then why's the phone off the hook, Elizabeth? Are you trying to cut yourself off from humanity completely?'

'Yes.'

He cocked his head and gazed at her sadly. 'Oh, come on, Elizabeth, I wasn't born yesterday. Alex was here and you're covering up for him.'

'No, but you think whatever you like.' She turned away from him as if indifferent but really to hide her eyes.

'So, you have someone new under your lovely blue wing,' he stated.

Relief flooded her; she collapsed onto her couch. 'Actually, I was just contemplating suicide and didn't want to be disturbed.' She wasn't really lying, because if Alex didn't come on Sunday that would definitely be her condition.

'Oh, baby, I'm sorry...' It was his soft, disarming tone, so that when he came and sat beside her she leaned against him and let him put his hand over hers on her knee.

'Oh, Jim,' she sighed.

He slipped his other hand beneath the heavy fall of her hair, caressing her soothingly. 'I'm sorry,' he whispered, lowering his face towards hers. 'You really are my sad, blue one. But you want too much out of life, Elizabeth. We were happy together, weren't we? You've had more than most people ever dream of, but you had to give it all up for an impossible fantasy, for an adolescent infatuation with a guitarist.'

'Shut-up, Jim.'

'I'm sorry,' he breathed, and turned her face towards his. He kissed her, shoving his tongue into her mouth, and its quivering probes made her think of a snake's rattling tail as he aimed for her throat. She tried to push him away, but his arm had become a vice around her shoulders while his hand gripped her face, his thumb pressing into her soft cheek arousing him by evoking the hardness of his cock buried in the deep warmth of her pussy. Then miraculously, the doorbell rang again. She shoved him away and ran to open the door.

Audrey was standing out on the landing, her burning gold hair cascading down over her slender arms and torso. 'I've been worried about you, Elizabeth,' she stated without preamble. 'I've been trying to call you for days.'

Elizabeth gratefully took her soft arm and pulled her into the room, hearing her exclaim, 'Oh!' when she saw Jim.

'She was just contemplating suicide and didn't want to be disturbed,' he informed her agreeably.

'Is that true?' Audrey turned to her, concerned.

'Don't worry about it.' Elizabeth was smiling at this wonderful coincidence.

Jim rose. 'See if you can talk her out of it, Audrey. Personally, I think she's a little too young to be so depressed. She should have the decency to wait until she starts losing her feminine charms, or until I stop financing her self-indulgence.'

He headed for the door but Elizabeth stopped him, grabbing his arm. 'We have to talk about that, Jim.' She wanted to be free of him.

'Some other time, sweet one. Put your phone back on the hook and I'll call you.' But he looked at her sadly for a long moment, until she was ready to throw her arms around his neck. Then abruptly he pulled her to him. With Audrey there she felt safe, so she satisfied her desire to give into a nostalgic sorrow for what they had had together. 'Why don't you tell her to go and let's make love,' he whispered in her ear. 'It can't hurt, for old time's sake, sweet one, you know how good it was...'

She pulled away, heaving an anguished sigh. 'No!' She stared into his dark eyes.

'Never again, blue one?' he asked softly, and it hit her suddenly that this pain was only a small glimmering of what Alex was going through with Linda. *He can't possibly leave her!* She thought. *He can't possibly love me!* her mind screamed, and then Jim was hovering before her terrifyingly, as if he was a vampire about to bite her neck, the red rug her blood gushing out and filling the room as she fell.

* * *

'What happened?' Elizabeth asked weakly. She only knew she was lying on her couch with Audrey beside her and that Jim nowhere in sight, but this all pleased her enough she lay there contentedly.

'You fainted,' Audrey told her, looking troubled.

'Oh...'

'I didn't know women fainted in real life, Elizabeth. What's going on?'

'Alex came the night of the day we went shopping.'

'No!'

'Yes. I was trying on what I had bought and he was suddenly at the door... He stayed with me four nights and three days. I took the phone off the hook while he was here and completely forgot about it.'

'It was that good, huh?' Audrey stated knowledgeably and Elizabeth nodded, grateful she didn't have to try and describe what she was experiencing. 'You haven't been eating, have you?'

She shook her head.

'That's why you passed out when you got upset.' She stood up, her bracelets clicking efficiently. 'I'm going to fix us some lunch and you're going to eat every bite, then we'll talk.'

'But Audrey, I can't do either one. I don't know what's going to happen!' Her voice wailed pathetically from the couch as if she was a banshee dying under the spell of a mortal man.

# Chapter Thirty-Two

Sunday. Elizabeth had half her closet strewn across her bed, the walls of her bedroom appropriately colorless for the pure, quiet morning. She was planning to take the whole day to decide what she was going to greet him in. It had to be casual because she was lying around the house, but also stunning because he was coming. Yet it seemed the night would never arrive. She felt she could go through all the clothing women have worn throughout history and it would still be this endlessly boring morning.

She didn't even have any dreams to entertain herself with because since Alex had come and gone she slept with the black heaviness of the dead every night as if her waking life was the dream now. Her only physical exertion was lifting a cup of tea to her lips. She strolled into her living room, sorry Audrey hadn't been able to spend the day with her, but she and Mario had already made plans. Jim hadn't called and she was glad. She didn't care about anything except what was happening with Alex because it determined whether or not she was going to live or die.

She stood over her disk player and caressed it lovingly. It was where her heart lived these days.

She put in a CD and strolled back into the bedroom to continue wading through her wardrobe – a sea of colors and textures – trying to decide which part of it he would experience tonight when she opened the world of her arms for him. Then she saw a dress and knew it was the one she had to wear, and she was only just a little upset she had made the decision so early in the day and had nothing else to do. She slipped it on – a black, long-sleeved, knee-length dress with a large red-and-gold butterfly embroidered over the chest, smaller ones flying around her legs on the skirt whose two folds opened up like wings. *This is it*, she thought, and took her time hanging everything back up after slipping off the dress and laying it reverently across the bed.

Now what? What if he doesn't come? Don't even think about that, not yet, wait until it's dark out, at least. She switched on the television to dim her mind and spirit to the point of nonexistence and rest from his presence inside her for a while.

\* \* \*

Sunday night, nine o'clock, found Elizabeth staring at her digital clock and feeling the figure of the 9 as herself with her head bent in fear trying not to look at the possibility of what might happen – that he might not come.

'I hate this!' she exclaimed out loud, rising and pacing her living room. 'I'm an absolutely useless creature! I haven't done anything all week but wait for him! Disgusting! But this is the turning point, I either live or die. How can you do anything when you're waiting for your sentence?' She stared at the door. 'All right, Alex, *now*!' Nothing happened. She sighed and sat back down.

\* \* \*

Monday morning. One minute after midnight found Elizabeth standing alone in the world, the mystery of the One that became two Alex and Linda, with no room for her. She couldn't believe he hadn't come, even though she was not at all surprised. But she hated the part of her that accepted it; the part of her who just sat there, dry-eyed, trying to coolly, rationally, talk herself out of suicide.

*I should have known. One week back with his wife and the weight of nine years crushed me out of his heart. It's not his fault; any man would have succumbed to the onslaught of my stupid dreams. I deserve this pain, after all, it's nothing compared to how Linda would have felt if he left her... Do I have any sleeping pills?*

She got up and headed for the kitchen cabinets, all the while knowing that she didn't, but hoping that some would materialize as divine compensation for the fact that he hadn't. But no, she found nothing except knives in a drawer, and she didn't want to kill the butterfly on her chest, only the pain.

'He didn't even call!' she moaned out loud. 'Oh, God, he didn't even call!' she sobbed, frightened that she couldn't cry as she walked slowly back into her living room. *He didn't even call...* The thought kept re-playing in her head. *He didn't come and he didn't even call.* She covered her temples with her hands trying not to hear the words, but the phrase kept repeating itself to the beat of her heart like the ticking of a time-bomb. She saw herself in her mind's eye weeping until she was so exhausted that she fell asleep and thought, *No! I'll just have to wake up again, I'm going to sleep for good. I've always considered this life a little ridiculous in its hardships and limitations, but without him it makes absolutely no sense at all.*

She wandered into her bathroom, vaguely thinking it had to contain some item useful for ending pain, traditionally a razor blade. She grimaced in distaste at the thought of being so unoriginal even while realizing that it was suicide itself that was trite no matter how she went about it. She stood beneath the bright light, gazing at herself in the mirror, the open butterfly like a wound in her chest symbolizing the paralyzed flight of her soul because he didn't love her. She saw him standing by the shower and squeezed her eyes closed from the stab of pain, thinking it should have been enough to kill her, and wishing it had. She didn't want to survive it, she didn't want to stop loving him, it was the only thing that made the world magical. But it was a two-edged sword, because without him it was hell.

She bent over the sink. *This is intolerable!* Her mind screamed. *I worship him!*

The door bell rang.

She raced out of the bathroom and didn't see anything, propelled by sheer joy.

She was in his arms and she couldn't believe it, his soft white suit jacket all the light in the universe, which had become his chest in a black shirt. Her body was trembling in his arms, as if the butterflies on her dress were literally flying around him.

'I wasn't going to come...' She heard him say as the damn of self control broke inside her from the rush of joy at his presence and she started to cry. 'I wasn't going to come...' he repeated and she could only cling to him. 'Elizabeth...'

'No!' she breathed, pulling him into her apartment, closing the door and hugging him again, perfectly content.

'We have to talk,' he said firmly, but she felt his mind quickly wandering with his hands. She opened the wings of her dress for him and they took off together, soaring above the painfully solid ground of circumstances in a kiss. She had purposefully not worn panties to be open to his fingers that she loved so much thrusting hungrily into her pussy.

'We have to talk, Elizabeth!' The angry urgency of his statement was in his hand now, transforming it into an intense pleasure without any meaning except itself so it didn't matter what he was saying.

'Yes!' she breathed, kissing his neck.

He pushed her away slowly. 'I can't stay...'

'You can't stay?' Her voice was barely audible, as if this might make the fact itself vanish.

He gripped her arms, staring into her eyes. 'No, I can't.'

'Did you tell Linda about us?' she asked, feeling that now she had nothing to lose by finally openly talking about what was happening. She hadn't done so before because it was beyond any possible words, and because she hated to put any sort of pressure on him, but now she was fighting for her life; if he left so soon it would kill her.

He let go of her, looking away, and she knew he hadn't told his wife about them. 'No,' he admitted with a lost look, glancing over his shoulder at the door as if trying to keep in mind that he had to leave.

She felt like embracing him and telling him to go because she couldn't stand to see him like that, but she wasn't sure that was what he really wanted, or she would have, without remembering what it would mean for her after he was gone.

'But she knows something's going on, especially after tonight she'll know. I shot out of the house literally at the stroke of midnight as if I was under a spell or something.'

'Really?' She smiled, liking the image so much she forgot for a moment the painful reality behind it. But everything always felt like a back-drop, a stage set, when he was present, there for the endless expression of their feelings for each other.

'Yes, really.' He looked at her and his eyes were so heavy that she fell on her knees before him, wrapping her arms around his hips and speaking softly.

'You don't have to tell her, Alex, she doesn't ever have to know... I just want you to come whenever you desire it without fighting it, because there's no reason to fight it. I only want to enhance your life...'

'But that changes it, don't you see?' He rested his hands on her head.

'Yes, I see. I see that I want to die if I think I'll never be with you again, that's all I see, that's all I know. It's wrong, I know it, but it doesn't change the way I feel about you, Alex.' She clung to him, terrified of his imminent departure.

He stroked her head gently. 'It's okay, I'm not leaving, and in the morning I'm going home and telling Linda the truth, that you're a witch!' He pulled her up into his arms and they didn't talk after that.

# Chapter Thirty-Three

'Come on, come on...' The waves of an orgasm began sucking his energy into her, her pussy clinging to his cock and urging it deeper into the contractions of her pleasure. But he always managed to escape, pulling his erection out of her climax, her heart pounding out of a love for him so intense and yet so fine it was the edge of a sword cutting through the surface of everything; penetrating to the core of the world and setting her on fire. They lay on their sides, kissing between each flight into the mysterious heart of the universe when he ejaculated violently inside of her. He stared at her, resting her cheek in his hand, large and sensitive and half consuming her face, her lips softly parted, always ready for his kisses, petulantly asking for them.

\* \* \*

They were sitting up in bed, his arm around her shoulders. 'I wanted to commit suicide tonight before you came,' she confessed, 'and the only reason I didn't is because it just seemed so horribly trite.'

'So that's why I shot over here as if all the devils in hell were after me!'

She laughed. 'Yes, the bells were tolling what would have been the final beats of my heart if you hadn't come.'

'You wouldn't really have killed yourself, Elizabeth.' He refused to even make this a question.

'I don't know…' she replied sincerely.

'Elizabeth…'

'You're right I wouldn't have, not while you were still on earth and there was the hope of seeing you again.'

'Do you love me?'

She glanced up at him, keeping her hand possessively on his chest. He was smiling down at her. 'I hate you,' she said, and they kissed for a while.

'I have to break it to Linda tomorrow,' he declared suddenly.

'Oh, God.' She winced at the pain in his voice and caressed him, knowing there was nothing she could say in those moments to make him feel better.

'How did this happen?' His hand gripped hers.

'Jim… that night at the restaurant…' She spoke softly, re-experiencing the vision of him at the bar. 'And then you were a bad little boy and wanted to see my dreams…'

'But if I had just looked at your paintings and left…'

'I'd feel the same way about you but still be unhappily engaged to Jim thinking you were only an implausible fantasy. And you would have missed your chance to live inside the arms of a priestess…'

'A priestess?'

'Yes, of Isis.'

'Tell me about her.'

'She is the principle ancient Egyptian goddess, the metaphysical force of woman, Osiris her brother and her lover, the spirit of man. They were the first king and queen, reigning in harmony at the dawn of the world. But then Seth, Osiris' evil brother who stands for mortality – the physical substance of which life is made that becomes corrupt if it's divorced from the divines spirit – murdered him and took over. He cut Osiris up into fourteen pieces and scattered them all over the earth so that Isis could never find him, and these pieces stand for the physical laws composing the experiential mystery of the world. But she did find them, journeying everywhere and putting him back together again with her love, which is the single unifying force behind the diversity of life. The only part of him she couldn't find was his penis, because Seth threw it into the Nile and a crocodile swallowed it. But it didn't matter, Isis spread the love wings of her soul over him and conceived their child Horus, the avenger of his father, the conscious integration of spirit and flesh who murders Seth, the cynical, unimaginative, loveless view of the world. And when Seth died, Osiris was reborn, and he and Isis reign as the wholeness of the universe and the creative polarity of life, and every human soul is their son, Horus. When Christianity took over the ancient religion, all that happened was that the story and the names were changed, but the spirit remained essentially the same – God, Osiris, Mary, Isis, and Horus, Jesus. And how did you like your ancient history lesson? I admit, it seems pretty gory roaming the world looking for the pieces of your lover, but it does correspond to a deep psychological root inside a woman's soul… the way her lover is only a mortal man at the mercy of the elements, yet in her soul he is all the universe, her love literally making him divine…'

Alex kissed her to shut her up, but she felt his deep gratification.

\* \* \*

They woke up in the morning when she rolled into his arms. They stared into each other's eyes, smiling, but then his brow darkened and she knew he had remembered Linda's pain.

'I should go,' he stated quietly, his hands exploring, rediscovering her, because no matter how many times he penetrated her body and claimed it for himself, the mood and depth of her feelings and of her pussy were always an exciting unknown.

'Yes,' she whispered, not wishing to prolong his painful

position, wanting him to move out of it as cleanly and swiftly as possible. She didn't know what he was going to do and she had no intention of asking him. He had said he wanted her and that was more than enough for her. She just hoped he would be quick about it once he plunged the knife in and not keep turning it over in his mind so he and Linda fell helplessly into each others arms again from the pain.

'Okay,' he said, waiting for her encouragement.

'Okay,' she echoed.

'Okay.'

Smiling, she bent over his lap and pleasantly moistened her dry tongue with the gentle froth of his semen as she sucked him down, waking him up with a loving blowjob.

Afterwards he sat up and kissed her where she knelt, then he got out of bed and began getting dressed with a ritual-like slowness that aroused and tormented her all at once.

She watched him from the bed, casually propped up on her pillows but terrified. *What if the same thing happens, that when he gets home he regrets it and decides never to come back again'?* She closed her eyes from the black weight that descended on her heart at the thought, and when she opened them again, he was ready to go.

He sat on the edge of the bed and stared at her, and she wanted to tell him that if he didn't come back very soon she would die without having to kill herself, because it would just happen naturally; her soul would wither away without him in the same inevitable way people die of old age. He took her hand and she pressed this knowledge into him.

'I'll be back tonight,' he said, and she nodded feeling absolutely blessed, as if she was going to be admitted into heaven after only one day of purgatory.

He got up and she started to rise to walk him to the door, but he pushed her back down gently, bending over her. 'No, you stay right here. I'll turn on the Recorder and you dream something beautiful for me.'

'I worship you,' she whispered, her dark eyes narrowed by a cat-like devotion to him.

He smiled and walked over to the Recorder.

'There's a blank DVD in it already,' she said and he turned on the machine.

'Now go to sleep,' he urged, 'and dream all day for me.' His eyes were heavy on her soul as he closed the door.

# PART TWO

# Chapter One

Elizabeth fully realized the erotic potential of every hotel room, each one essentially the same like the sex organs, but always varying in mood and quality like the act itself. It had become her art, her sensuality flowing instead of paints and making of each normal, objective space a magically sensual realm where the heavy, routine chain of time fell away from them and they were freed into the eternal pulse of pleasure. Nothing to her was without a profound meaning, a metaphysical dimension that freed it from the limited solidity which she felt was the root of boredom. For example, walking into their latest hotel room, she perceived the narrow entrance hall as the slender length of his penis and the open space of the room beyond it as her womb. She smiled thinking this as the bellhop set their suitcases down. Alex tipped the young man and he left politely dazzled.

*Young people are taught to respect specific kinds of people like politicians and war heroes ,she thought, studying her surroundings contentedly. But there's usually nothing admirable about them as far as a true reverently creative enjoyment of life is concerned.*

She sighed happily, drawing open a curtain over a glass door leading out onto a balcony as Alex collapsed onto the bed, and his groan seemed to fill the gray afternoon sky for her. She quickly closed the curtain again and turned to him.

He grinned at her, chewing on a piece of gum, and she began subtly trembling inside remembering her first time with him; recalling the fear of never seeing him again that had made his penetrations feel painfully deep. She still couldn't believe that his presence – which was such an earth-shattering joy for her – could remain a constant without killing her. On the contrary, its wonder increased in intensity and she responded to it as deeply, but with growing self-confidence, more and more able to please him as much as he devastated her. Whatever he felt she felt, and was doubled in intensity by her response.

She was developing the theory that a man's personality is reflected in his love-making, how he lives how he loves. Alex's almost religious devotion to his music turned her on as much or more than his strong, sexy body. She loved the way he concentrated and exercised his technical skills on his guitars, constantly changing chords without hesitating and losing the rhythm, an art he transferred to the living instrument of her body, veined for his feeling like a guitar for his touch. The freedom with which he moved on stage holding his instrument was the way he moved inside of her holding her body in his arms, positioning her with the same swift passion he changed chords, imbuing endlessly different moods to the flow of their pleasure. Each of their unions was like a song, mysteriously different in the depth and force and rhythm of his penetrations, yet always the same in its intense spirit of love as all songs are music.

She knelt at the foot of the bed and removed his shoes, throwing them onto the rug with a gentle thud that was hauntingly erotic; evoking the deep, quiet sound of his body beating against hers. She pulled off his other shoe with the smoothness of his sex sliding out of hers. Everything was arousing for her in his presence, and when she touched him a haze immediately covered her awareness like the film over a fish's eye, her surroundings beginning to dissolve in the pleasure that immediately flowed through her body. Without him she would be stranded in an existential void like a fish out of water.

His smile dimmed into a soft, consenting gaze as he watched her opening his pants. She wanted him to relax, so she moved with a dream-like slowness, sensing how her gentle touches gradually hypnotized him.

She kissed his stomach, trying not to let its firmness arouse her so much that her movements lost their fairy-like gentleness.

He sat up abruptly and pulled off his shirt, falling back against the pillows with his eyes closed, and she was overjoyed to feel the complete submission of his body.

She covered him with kisses light as dandelion seeds filled with a life-time of desire that had come true in him. She crouched over his body without touching it and kissed his brow, softly blowing the wheat-golden strands of hair away and covering his eyelids with her lips so that he would perceive her caresses as the whole world, her touch its laws that were there only for his pleasure. She kissed his tender boy's cheeks but only brushed his lips with hers, afraid of falling into him with the weight of her desire. She then returned to the precious area where his feeling was concentrated.

He raised his hips off the bed so she could remove his pants, and she tossed them away with the complete lack of concern for everything except him that was her natural state. She took his cock into her mouth gently, maternally moved by its vulnerable softness, yet passionately aroused by its almost indifferent coolness. She washed the wave of her tongue over him in a slow, soothing rhythm, holding the base of his penis gently with her fingertips while her other hand explored the deep warmth of his thigh, enjoying the friction of his flesh against her palm, becoming more electrical with each caress. She sensed the slow surging of his blood towards his erection deliciously filling her mouth. She licked him more hungrily, gently launching his full length completely between her lips so his swelling head grazed her throat. Then she sat up to look at his penis pointing blindly upward. Her senses took off with him as she gripped it firmly and caressed him, her rhythm slowly quickening. She lightly licked his head, then gently placed it between her lips again and squeezed his balls to feel its upward thrust. She took her time because she loved the wonderfully arduous task of making him come in her mouth.

# Chapter Two

Alex was warming up for the concert, playing his classical guitar as Elizabeth lay naked on the bed, curled up and watching him. His quiet, thoughtful plucking, and sensual, rhythmic strumming, lulled her into a state of perfect contentment. She was filled with an exquisite peace so unknown to her she felt as though she was in another dimension. There was no populated hotel around them; they were in the isolated tower of an enchanted castle. There was no traffic-ridden, pollution-filled city below them; there was only inviolate nature blooming with virginal innocence as the seeds of his notes fell into the deep soil of her heart, the space of the world opening up like her arms to hold him. She knew that factory towers rose in the grey distance like the pipes of an infernal organ, but no matter how demonic, they were still music in his presence. Because without this industry there would be none of the equipment that literally blew her away at every one of his concerts, and no Dream Recorders with which to have won his love. The factory towers were magical wands currently in the hands of evil wizards, blindly selfish and visionless, but they were still magic.

He was naked, lovingly holding his instrument, and after a while she felt jealous of it and wanted to pull it away from him and replace it with her body. But she didn't, knowing that now

*Moonlit Dreams*

he was with his music. She lay perfectly still and silent, hoping that he would feel her soul, her love for him, flowing inside the music and surrounding him.

She still didn't know if she was going with him to the concert hall tonight she was so exhausted. Because every time she went she danced almost the whole time, she had to. The music lifted her up like his arms positioning her when they were making love, and once she began moving in rhythm with it she couldn't stop. She didn't just jump around like a live wire with too much current flowing through it, she tried to embody the different moods of his guitar with the different parts of her body, trying to become them, to feel the music descend into her like naked energy into clothing. It was as if she became the flesh of his spirit, really feeling him inside of her, not just between her legs with his body beating against hers.

Dancing at his concerts took a lot out of her, so she didn't know if she was going tonight. After all, there were so many concerts left; they would be on the road for weeks. She licked her lips, too content to get up for a drink of water, and stretched, extending her arms and legs before her like a cat. Then she curled up again, looking over at him.

He was smiling at her, watching her now as he kept playing.

*I'll stay here and bring out the mood of this room,* she thought. They were leaving in the morning, but even if he only experienced it for ten minutes when he walked in after the concert before falling asleep, it would be worth it. No effort was too great for even one moment of his pleasure. She smiled over at him, wondering what she could do with this space. Most hotel rooms were so plain; no matter how cheap or expensive they were there was nothing creatively sensual about them, only sexually comfortable. But wherever they went, and no matter how little time they stayed, she created worlds for him. She had atmospheric equipment tucked away in her suitcases, magical little treasures created by the wizard wands of the factory towers, and the rest involved making imaginative use of the room's raw material. *Which, she thought, is crude indeed.*

He gazed down at his guitar again and her mind wandered, unable to think about anything but the fact that she wanted him to look at her as he played.

'Why don't you finish warming up your fingers with me?' she teased him quietly.

He looked back at her seriously, his hair falling over his forehead a sunlit curtain over the stage of flesh which for her heart was the whole world, each one of their lives on earth a hauntingly unique script. And for a moment she regretted saying it, a stab of jealousy for his guitar slowing down her heart, but then he suddenly lifted it off him.

Her body instantly began quivering with suspense. 'Just pretend I'm another one of your guitars...' Her voice was barely there as he sat on the edge of the bed and rested his hand on her womb in a natural, instinctive gesture, smiling into her eyes.

'Well, first of all you need strings.'

'My veins are my strings, silly!' She lay on her back before him and extended her arms stiffly above her head, resting the back of one hand on the palm of another. 'That's the neck,' she told him. 'And where your hand is is the sound box.'

'And what are they?' He smiled down at her legs.

'Oh, well, they're just the stand.'

'Mm...' He put his hands gently on her thighs and spread them open. 'What a strange guitar,' he commented. He touched her labial lips curiously. 'Oh, my God,' he whispered as if in shock, 'it's wet. It'll get ruined.' He slipped a finger inside her pussy and she closed her innermost flesh around him hungrily, moaning. 'Well, it still has a nice sound, anyway.' He pulled her up into his arms.

She kept her arms straight above her head as he turned her to the side and held her against him, his right hand resting comfortably between her thighs. 'What a nice, soft guitar,' he whispered. 'With invisible inner strings, and all warm and moist where you play it…' He caressed her vulva gently, so that she made soft, quiet sounds. She was already in danger of coming from the joy of being held by him and from his palm rubbing firmly against her clitoris. 'This is how you strum it.' He continued his observations with a contained, quiet air as if talking to himself.

'Oh, stop… stop!' she breathed.

'Guitars don't talk,' he said firmly, but he stopped caressing her and vibrated her sensitive folds of skin with his fingertips. 'This is how you pluck it, and you definitely wouldn't want to use a pick.'

She let out a long, low moan.

'What a haunting tone,' he commented coolly, and let her have his finger again. Her pussy sucked on it with a blind, desperate hunger, her mind as blank as an infant knowing only a silent screaming need for him. 'And it gives off such a wonderful, intoxicating scent.' He suddenly slipped another finger inside her.

She gasped as he penetrated her rhythmically with his hand.

'Oh, wonder of wonders!' he whispered, and she began to climax from the joy of being the object of his fascination. 'It's both a wind *and* a string instrument.' He pushed his fingers harder and deeper into her pussy, the base of his palm firmly caressing her clit as he felt the contractions of her orgasm. She abandoned her guitar shape and clung to his wrist emitting one low, sustained cry as the ecstasy played itself out inside her.

He held her tenderly for a moment then spread her back across the bed and kissed her forehead. 'I have to get ready.' He moved away from her into the room and she lay with her eyes closed peacefully.

'Are you coming?' he asked.

'I just did.' She smiled.

# Chapter Three

Alex was gone, playing in a vast concert hall, his body temporarily the property of countless people – thousands of live wires through which the powerful energy of his music was flowing and charging them with positive feelings. Elizabeth knew this was so, because when she first heard his music it made her feel positive about life again. She bought his first CD, then another one and another one. *Then the second miracle happened,* she thought, awakening to her surroundings again. *Alex entered my life in the flesh.*

She pictured him in the concert hall and at the same time wondered what she could do with this room, thinking that she really didn't have the energy to do anything. But she wanted to, because in the morning they would be on the bus again, and comfortable as it was there were other people around, so that every moment alone with him was precious. The hardships of road life exemplified for her the limitations of mortality that still remained despite the power of their love.

She closed her eyes, falling asleep and dreaming that she was in the concert hall watching him from the darkness of the wings and dancing.

*  *  *

Elizabeth loved the concept of modern physics that if a theory fails it's because it isn't beautiful enough. That was how she felt about Jim and the time when she thought she loved him. It had failed between them because the feelings for each other hadn't been deep enough; they had

been in love mainly with the idea of their love. But Alex's eyes were like lazer beams that cut through her mind and reached straight to her heart – how she felt about him was first, and what she thought about this feeling was second and ultimately irrelevant. With Jim it had been the reverse. She had fueled her desire for him with her admiration of his intelligence, but with Alex her respect was the by-product of how completely he devastated her emotionally; there was nothing cerebral about her embrace of him. In his arms she felt herself a pure reality – her love for him. It didn't matter that he never said awesomely profound things like Jim had, that they never engaged in stimulating conversations about the unfathomable, divine nature of life, because they were experiencing and proving it with their love.

Elizabeth knew to give him his own space, especially on the bus when they couldn't be alone anyway. At first it had shocked her profound mentality to see him comfortably slumped in his seat watching television as the world flew by outside with the same swift unreality as the changing scenes on the screen. *He's not thinking anything deep*, she thought, for a split second wondering if she had been wrong and it was really with Jim she could get along; that it was really Jim who felt things as intensely as she did. But the thought disintegrated in the magnetic electricity of Alex's blue eyes when he smiled at her. She took his hand and kissed it with the sorrowful feeling of apologizing to his spirit, which she had momentarily desecrated with her conceptual doubt. He looked back at the TV again and forgot her, but she didn't care anymore, he was all that mattered.

*All his thoughts are in his touch, he doesn't have to waste his time conceptualizing about the mystery of the universe, he's in perfect harmony with it through his music, possessing a wordless understanding of its nature through his continual enjoyment of, and controlled devotion to, his self-expression.*

She gazed at his profile, glad he was oblivious to her because in those moments she felt like a floating mind, painfully removed from her body and any real contact with life.

*Oh, God, how I need him!*

She closed her eyes as she felt her soul deliciously curling up like a cat in the wonder of her flesh through the warm feel of his hand in hers.

*I'll take care of all the deep thinking for him, because just his glance, his mere touch, turns on all these incredible thoughts inside me about the miraculous nature of reality.*

She rested her head on his arm and started falling asleep, feeling their two seats on the bus as the heart of the universe on an endless journey into itself...

She began dreaming, still half awake, conscious not only of his presence against her but also of the entourage of the road crew that surrounded them. Alex treated her like a queen before them.

Elizabeth knew his divorce had been made easier for him by the fact that Linda had been more enraged than heart-broken. She had put up with his life-style for years, staying at home with their son while he toured the country, and now he wasn't coming back at all, which made of her emotional investment in him one without any profit, not counting the lavish alimony he bestowed on her.

*He was away from the nest so much anyway*, Elizabeth thought. *She should have known he'd fly away for good one day when he met a woman with creative wings as powerful as his own.*

And Jim had freed her from him with an amazingly good-natured attitude. 'I'm proud of you, Elizabeth,' he had said. 'You made something completely implausible a reality...'

On this remembered note, she drifted off.

# Chapter Four

*R*oad life is getting to me, she thought. *Everything gets to me after a while, I wasn't born with a single drop of ability to deal with routine; everything bores me right away.*

She was lying on the bed of yet another hotel room, watching Alex prepare for yet another concert, and the thought of boarding the bus again in the morning made her absolutely weary. She could still feeling its perpetual motion through what seemed like empty space, because every city was essentially the same.

Yet the concerts she still enjoyed as much, or even more, as the first one. Each time she went to one of his performances her body felt more and more like a virginal membrane the music was thrusting against until by the end it seemed to have broken through to the ecstatically fluid core of her being. She experienced a state of perfect fulfillment that was beyond words in the same way she couldn't think during orgasm. And Alex was always smiling afterwards, gleaming with sweat that made him look even more luminous to her. She imagined that to him and the other members of the band performing was like making love. Even if they were tired, as they often were towards the end of a tour, they were never half-hearted about it. She knew the chords had become a mechanical routine for his fingers, but she also knew that his feeling was always in them.

He grinned at her where she sat slumped in a chair with the

limp air of a rag doll, the dressing room realistically bright after the haunting darkness of the wings from where she watched him play. Then people began flowing in like a river and she didn't even try to get close to him in those moments. She usually went back to the hotel room when she had the strength to move again. Unless Mike, the drummer, came and sat beside her and they started talking, then she didn't leave. She and Mike had gotten along from the first moment they met, their dark eyes flashing into each other's with the same degree of intelligence, a current of empathy flowing between them. They often sat together on the bus to talk. Mike completely satisfied the verbal, conceptual part of her, so that when she walked down the bus isle back to Alex, she was even more able to appreciate the silence of his smile and fall into his arms feeling the universe was coming around her and holding her in its divine safety, so that she no longer had to defend her heart with thoughts.

'Are you coming?' Alex asked and she opened her eyes. She had been lost in the flowing images of their life like her body on the endless flow of the highway. Suddenly she thought she would scream from the monotonous repetition of this scene, but fortunately, or unfortunately, she didn't know which, she was too tired.

'No,' she said, but as he turned away she broke down. 'Oh, God, Alex, I can't stand the thought of getting on that bus again in the morning! I just can't!'

He sat on the bed beside her and she immediately relaxed. 'You don't have to. We'll stay here a few more nights then take a plane. I need a break, too.'

She looked up at him, too happy to say anything.

'Will you let me rest?' he whispered, kissing her.

'Yes,' she lied, smiling.

\* \* \*

She didn't let him rest, so he revenged himself. He knelt and penetrated her from behind but didn't move. With one hand he played with her breasts while with the other hand he held her down against the bed, gripping the back of her neck when she tried to rise, impaling her on his cock and taking his pleasure from her vaginal walls clenching around his motionless hard-on as she moaned for mercy. But he remained implacably still in the wound of her feeling for him, slowly draining all her energy as she struggled against him, trying to reach a climax and end the exquisite torture. She was close to sobbing from the effort she was making to come and from his distance; deliriously feeling like an animal caught in a hunter's trap set in the trunk of a tree. Yet knowing that she was feeding his pleasure with her struggles stoked her own excitement. She desperately wanted to reach his hand playing idly with her breasts and tried to catch it in hers so she could bring it to her lips and experience the mysterious aspects of his personality embodied in his fingers. He seemed to know what she wanted because he suddenly cupped her face with one hand and let her tongue play passionately with his thumb, yet still he continued tormenting her with the crystallization of his erection deep in her pussy.

'Talk to me, at least!' she gasped.

He pulled her up against him, his hard arm a vice against her soft body. 'Talk to you?' he muttered, and her head fell back against his shoulder longing for his kiss, but he wouldn't give it to her. 'Talk to you?' he repeated incredulously, but she barely heard him over her own cries, her body heaving like sob against his implacability.

He let her go just as abruptly and she fell forward on the bed again. It was as if her soul left her body when his cock slid out of her. She quickly rolled onto her back and he gripped her behind the knees, pushing them slowly up to her shoulders with the weight of his body while. She gazed at his penis in a trance as he held it over her begging hole.

'Do you want it?' he whispered, kissing her neck and then

her lips and cheeks distractingly, so that she closed her eyes in a frustrated agony of pleasure. She reached up and feverishly stroked his hair, trying to calm herself with its cool softness while biting his lips, wanting to devour him now that she almost had him. He dipped the very tip of his erection inside her but sidetracked her again with a long, violent kiss, and she responded passionately, getting all she could of him this way, the mouth of her sex sucking on his head contentedly. Then with a gradualness that stunned her with its unexpected generosity, he let her have the full length of his cock. He was holding her down so she couldn't rise up to meet him. She waited breathlessly for the touch of his body, and when she finally felt it her clitoris ruptured instantly. She climaxed in what felt like annihilating slow motion between her mouth and her sex as he kissed her gently.

'Oh, yes, yes!' she gasped.

He fucked her fast and hard, and her pleasure was profoundly heightened when she felt him coming with her, the waves of their mutual orgasm invisibly crashing against the walls of the room.

She caressed his hair and his face and kissed his neck and chest as he lay back smiling at her. She was experiencing a feverish rush of gratitude for the incredible pleasure he had given her, its tormenting quality forgotten in the intensity of the fulfillment. And she found herself thinking that higher beings often hold you to circumstances as he had her body to certain positions to deepen your appreciation for life. She wanted to communicate this idea to him because it was her desire to give him the world, and the only way to do so was to harness it in her thoughts. After all, the space of this life was brief, its dimensions were like a room they would soon be leaving, and she had no intention of losing him to the pure elements raging outside. The power of her perception was a vehicle she kept fueling for them. She kissed the soft flesh above his sex as he reached for the phone.

'What would you like for dinner, miss... what's your name?'
She licked her lips and kissed his still firm penis.

'Oh, no, you've had enough of that!' With his free hand he grasped her wrist and she obediently curled up against him while he called Room Service.

# Chapter Five

'You know we have a place when we get back,' he told her. 'I went out and looked at it before we left without telling you. It's a surprise.'

They were eating over the small table Room Service had rolled up. He had waited for her to finish her glass of wine before breaking the news to her, so that the knowledge entered her on its euphoric flow through her body. 'Oh, Alex, really?'

'Yes, really,' he responded quietly, and she glanced down at her food shyly. He took her hand and kissed her palm, urging her to look up at him again. He stared into her eyes and she felt the blood rushing through her heart. 'What are you thinking, Elizabeth? I would like to know.' His voice was so soft she distinctly felt the force of his desire within it. He let go of her hand and she lowered her head shyly again.

'I can't describe it...' she hedged.

'Try.'

She became confused from the combination of fear and excitement aroused in her by his willpower seeking to penetrate her imagination. He had never asked her to give herself to him in this way. 'It wouldn't make any sense if I just said it, Alex. It's my feelings for you rushing through my head in different images that try to express it... and they do, yet they don't, which is why they're always changing... because how I feel about you is the reality behind everything... the only thing that will never change...'

He smiled. 'Describe some of these images to me, Elizabeth. You haven't dreamed anything for me in a long time.'

'Oh, Alex!' She wanted to push the table away from between them, but instead sat paralyzed from the intensity of the love she felt for him. But then with the uncanny power he possessed in this respect, he fulfilled her wish as he stood up and offered her his hand. He led her over to the bed and she watched him arranging the pillows.

'Lie back on them,' he requested quietly.

She embraced him passionately, resting from his eyes that were always penetrating her; her soul constantly in a state of imaginative arousal his stare mysteriously plunged her into. Then she obeyed him, gazing up at him and watching him inexplicably walk over to his suitcase.

She was wearing a lace black negligee, her arms and legs pale and soft, and he was naked except for black silk shorts. He approached her again holding a black velvet jewel case with a casual reverence that took her breath away. He sat on the edge of the bed facing her. 'If you tell me what you were seeing, I'll give you a present.' He smiled, but his eyes retained the seriousness that turned her on so much. It was tormenting not to be able to give into him immediately with her body.

She focused on the soothing velvet darkness of the case as she spoke. 'I saw myself as a mermaid rising out of the water into your arms. My soul was the ocean and your spirit was the sun and its warm light sparkling on the were my thoughts, all about you... my long, flowing hair the never-ending darkness of the universe adorned with starfish and pearls like worlds created for your pleasure...' She looked back up at him. 'That's what I saw...' Her heart seemed to stop beating for an instant, the expression in his eyes almost frightening her, so that she felt she would die if he didn't tell her what he was thinking.

'Now isn't that funny, pearls and starfish did you say?'

'Yes!' she breathed, gazing at the black case feeling it was about to explode as he opened it.

'Look what we have here.'

Her eyes widened incredulously as she saw a necklace of pearls and star-shaped rubies resting against the black velvet.

'It must have materialized when you thought about it,' he concluded matter-of-factly.

'Oh, my God, Alex!'

'Well, since it's here, you might as well put it on.'

'Oh, Alex!'

He set the case aside and held the necklace up for her. 'You have a powerful imagination, Elizabeth.' He didn't smile as he rested the pearls and stars on the black lace over her chest, admiring them as he fastened the necklace behind her neck, and her eyes closed from the blinding wonder of what was happening as reflected in his expression. 'Beautiful,' he whispered, his hands covering her breasts and then following the curves of her body. She gripped the back of his neck possessively with both hands and he allowed her to pull his head down to kiss him. But he kept it light, drawing back. 'We have to discuss this, Elizabeth. When we're touring Europe your imagination is going to get me into big trouble with customs. No, listen to me, you have to control yourself. You don't want me getting arrested, do you?'

She moaned as her desire was painfully heightened by the image of him being taken away from her. 'No, but I didn't materialize it in your suitcase. You bought it first and I saw it in your eyes when you were looking at me, because you were planning to give it to me tonight...'

'Oh, in that case, I'll have to stop looking at you.' He turned his face away.

'No, look at me!' she begged, but he kept teasing her until he couldn't take it himself.

* * *

They lay in each others arms drifting off, dark green waves of light flowing over them and through the room as if they were lying at the bottom of the ocean, the vertically striped sheets of the bed (which Elizabeth had thought absolutely horrendous when she first saw them) transformed into the grooves of a seashell in which they lay as one flesh.

She had set up her atmospheric equipment and now the blank gray screen of the television at the foot of the bed was transformed into a tunnel of light and dark circles spiraling into infinity and imbuing the open space of the room with a haunting timelessness. It was as if they were at the other end of a black hole, at the heart of the theoretical white hole that spews out everything it's cosmic partner has swallowed – all the dreams and ideas that life absorbs without seeming to give anything back creating their own magical reality on the other side of the universe, the distance only as thin as their flesh.

She was thinking intently. *When we're dead, we won't need suitcases or atmospheric equipment, everything will be contained in our love.*

Her thoughts never ceased because they were all concerned with her desire to remain with him after death supposedly parted them. She felt that was where the imaginative creativity of their love would reign unchecked, its power symbolized on earth by the creation of a physical life through the union of their bodies.

*In death our imaginations will embrace and bring worlds to life.*

She had received the image of stars and pearls from his mind as he held her hand and stared at her from across the table, and in her heart she knew the miraculous implications of this, but consciously it was beyond her ability to deal with yet.

She had always believed in the occult side of life, but now she knew it was real, because in her love for Alex she actually experienced its power...

She woke up suddenly in her bedroom. The wall panels were colorless the way they had been all day Sunday and after he arrived at midnight when she had been to involved in him to care about them.

*Wait a minute,* she thought, *what's going on?* She saw that the Dream Recorder was turned on. *He told me to dream for him... oh, my God!*

Her body felt like lead; she couldn't move.

*I was dreaming! Touring with him was all a dream! He's still with Linda! What time is it?*

She somehow managed to turn her head to look at her digital clock.

Twelve midnight.

*And he didn't come back this time! He didn't come back!*

She tried to sit up, feeling as though she was being crushed by an unendurable weight of sorrow slowly pressing down on her.

*I slept all this time dreaming for him like he asked me to, but he doesn't love me! He stayed with Linda and everything that happened was a dream... touring with him, dancing in the wings, sitting beside him on the bus and talking to Mike, making love with him in all those different rooms, all of it was only a dream!*

'And the necklace!' she cried out loud. 'The necklace was just a dream!' She began sobbing, thinking that she had to be able to get up in order to kill herself.

'Elizabeth?'

Something jolted inside her and she thought it was her heart leaping out of the burning agony like someone from a building being consumed. Then everything was all right again as she realized the reason she couldn't move was because Alex was holding her in his arms.

# Chapter Six

Alex and Elizabeth were staying at her apartment while they furnished their new home. He gave her full reign over the decor, and their first day back in town she spent in front of her Dream Recorder collecting ideas from her dreams, which often had opulent settings, each item of furniture a work of art. Alex was out attending to arcane legal matters, so she called Audrey and asked her to come over to help her plan her dream home.

'This is going to cost a fortune, Elizabeth, to have everything custom made.' Ariana's carefree tone belied her sober observation.

'Alex has money, and besides, he told me I could have anything I wanted.' They were pouring through books on ancient cultures and tearing out pictures of particularly beautiful items.

'You should have asked for the Taj Mahal.'

'I have it, Audrey! The living room is going to be cosmic.'

'Let's hear it.'

'The couch is going to be soft black leather held together by silver stars. That's simple enough.'

'Yes...'

'Then the chairs around it are going to be hybrids of several ancient Egyptian models. One will have fold-out legs carved and painted to look like the long neck and beak of a bird, with the seat and back its soft wings. Another one will have the golden legs and paws of a leopard with a black and white tiger's pelt...'

'Nice. Go on.'

'You don't think it's outlandish, do you?'

'No, on the contrary, it's very organic.'

'Yes, and they're going to be exquisitely comfortable, just like a real bird's wings would be. And the three tables – two small ones beside the couch and a large one in front of it – are going to be of pure white alabaster because it's so smooth, and luminous and heavy, evoking the pure, stellar origins of the human skeleton...'

'Elizabeth, you're crazy!' Audrey laughed happily. 'Go on.'

'I haven't figured out the lamps that are going to go on the two small tables, but there'll be a deep, dark green area rug...'

'Like the earth.'

'Yes! And the curtains are going to be a luminous sky-blue... I think I'll have two crescent-shaped lamps on black stands on either side of the couch. So, how do you like it so far?'

'Cosmic, absolutely cosmic. But are you sure you don't just want a conventional white and silver living room set?' she teased.

'Oh, please, I don't want to live in a clinic. Besides, I want to confuse Alex... When he walks in I want him to feel like he just walked out into the sensual forces of the cosmos and that everything exists for his pleasure... the soft, deep universe couch where he can sit and read by the light of the moon... or lie and dream with his body surrounded by stars so I can look at him...'

'Oh, Elizabeth, how beautiful, you really love him.'

'I worship him. But I think maybe I should make the curtains black to go with the couch, the universe folding into the dimensions of a room, of time and space... What do you think?'

'No, too morbid, you need to lighten the metaphysical mood just a bit. What about the bedroom?'

'No, wait, we still have the den and the dining room…'

'I want to hear about the bedroom.'

'All right… it's going to be oceanic. The bed is going to be an open violet seashell, the top half the post, the bottom the frame holding the mattress, which will have to be round and large…'

'To allow for plenty of action.'

'Of course… and there'll be a white carpet with the smooth look of sand. Color panels for the walls, naturally, and the bathroom leading off it will have a seashell toilet, starfish faucet handles, and sea-green walls painted with beautiful exotic fish.'

'Lovely!'

'I don't know about the dresser though. I was thinking of making it a sunken treasure chest, dark wood and gold, but I don't know how that would look with the sand-white carpet and violet sea shell bed…'

'I don't like it.'

'No, me neither, it doesn't mean anything metaphysically; pirates and sunken treasures are a cultural phenomena. I'll just keep the one I have with color panels and get another one for Alex. And of course my Dream Recorder and screen are going in the room.'

'Well, obviously. Okay, now you can tell me about the den and the dining room.'

'Oh, God, no, I'm exhausted, let's eat.'

'I'll fix us something.'

'Great.'

Elizabeth was always delighted to eat whatever Audrey, who was macrobiotic, prepared for her. She always felt so good afterwards and wished she had the discipline to change her diet. The principle behind macrobiotics – balancing the Ying and Yang elements of the food to maintain a natural state of health – made perfect sense to her.

'The problem, Audrey, is that we're not raised with any sense of responsibility or balance,' she mused out loud watching the other woman cook. 'I mean, I literally grew up thinking food came from supermarkets. I remember the strange, guilty feeling of awe I experienced when it first dawned on me that those cold limbs I so casually extracted from clean, inorganic plastic used to be a warm, feathery, moving thing.'

'Oh, Elizabeth!' Audrey laughed as she moved about the kitchen with an efficient swiftness. 'Describe the den to me.'

'Well, I see it as a microcosm of the earth just as the living room is one of the cosmos and the bedroom of the ocean.'

'Uh-huh.'

'I need your ideas on this one, I'm much more of a space and ocean person, solid land is not my favorite place…'

'That makes sense, Elizabeth, 'cause you're really out there.'

'Is that a put down?' She smiled.

'No way.' Audrey grinned. 'I can't wait to experience your place.'

# Chapter Seven

It was raining outside. Alex was contentedly playing his guitar while Elizabeth stared out the window, feeling the impending melancholy of old age in the gray sky, the sun sorrowfully distant as one day his youth would be. But his blue eyes would still be the sky over the realm of all her dreams, their imaginations eternally limber. She sighed because this thought was only a slight consolation. Glancing back at him in the soft lamplight of her apartment, in her eyes he was still a boy made adorable by his single-minded devotion to his playing, and yet faster than the blink of an eye he would be an old man. One day she would be standing by a window looking out at another sad, rainy day, and when she turned around he would also be gray. How could she prevent the sun of positivism and joy vanishing from her soul with his golden head from the vision of her heart?

She sighed again and he looked over at her.

'Why don't you stop depressing yourself looking out at the rain,' he suggested.

His simple wisdom made her smile. 'But it's not the rain that's depressing me,' she drew the blinds, 'it's the thoughts it evokes.'

'Don't get intellectual with me, Elizabeth. Come here.' He set his guitar down.

'But Alex...' She hurried over to him, desperate to comfort herself with his indisputable wonder, his firm embrace sealing her in the moment and shutting out the debilitating abstractions of the future and death. 'I don't...' She couldn't finish, because nothing was wrong when she was holding him.

'You don't what?' he whispered, playing with her hair.

'Never mind, I'm a fool to be thinking these things. It'll always be you no matter what.' She smiled at him. 'My emotions were being Newtonian. I'm all right now. It'll always be your spirit no matter what happens to your flesh clothing.' She traced his lips with a fingertip, and the subtle sensation electrified her blood. She was always instantly charged with desire just by looking at his mouth, its expressions shooting off almost painful sparks of joy in her heart.

'My flesh clothes?' He smiled and bit her finger gently.

She was wearing a long white house dress covered with violet sprinkles of paint converging into an explosion of color over her sex. It opened all the way up the front, held together only by a thin black belt. He slipped his hands into the palette over her pussy, grinning at this area of utter devastation to her mind and his role in its demise. He literally took her consciousness in his hand and dissolved her thoughts with its motion, so that the profound sadness she had been feeling became a correspondingly deep physical pleasure.

'I'll make you feel better,' he promised her softly, and fell to his knees before her as if swearing to it.

She spread her legs and caressed his hair in rhythm with the waves of pleasure that began lapping gently around the boyish playfulness of his tongue circling her clitoris then swimming in the wet heart of her pussy, diving in more deeply as he gripped the soft, round cliffs of her hips. She moaned, entranced by the nearly cosmic beauty of his blonde hair over his black sweater. There was no external reality anymore; everything was being sucked into the dimensionless whirlpool of pleasure created by the knowledgeable spiraling of his tongue.

He stood up, filling her with a hungry sense of power, because those were her juices glistening with the warmth of starlight on his lips. She lifted his sweater urgently and he pulled it off, graciously offering her the warm, solid rays of his arms and chest enflaming the seed of her heart so that she twined herself like a plant around him, absorbing the heat of his skin. Meanwhile he undid his pants, and she almost swooned at his divine generosity. It was her turn to fall to her knees before him, and as she peeled off the useless skin of his pants. She slipped his cock between her lips and sucked on him fervently. He didn't say anything, which told her just how readily he received her worship, and this filled her with such happiness that she reached around and pushed him all the way into her mouth, feeling all her thoughts wash away in the overflow of fulfillment.

After a few minutes of enjoying her passionate blow-job, he pulled her to her feet and flung away her belt, lifting open the folds of her dress and gazing at the feast of her body before he began consuming it hungrily, licking and biting her breasts with starved violence, her back arching as she pushed her tender mounds exultantly into his mouth. And he responded to her supple submissiveness with a growing appetite, the more she gave him the more he took.

'Come on!' He pulled her into the bedroom and knelt on the bed as she lay before him. Urging her gently onto her side, he lifted her thigh and entered her from behind, snuggling passionately against her and stirring up deep waves of love for him in her womb.

'Oh, Alex...' She twisted her body around to meet his lips, parting her lips with the same languidness she opened her pussy up for him, relishing the combined penetrations of his cock and his tongue both thrusting into her. His swift, deep stabs were already making her come, and she tried controlling the intensity of her response with a growing languor. But then he groaned and the sound weakened her too profoundly to fight back a blooming orgasm. She would have climaxed but he suddenly pulled out of her, leaving her at the trembling point of death, the whole world balancing between her legs ready to crash and break apart into pure bliss.

'God, I love you!' he said angrily, and when his erection sank into her shamelessly wet pussy again it was the end for her.

# Chapter Eight

Elizabeth was thinking about the days before she heard Alex's music, the lonely feeling of possessing a sense others didn't, and the hopelessness of ever finding a man whose pure intensity would penetrate to the depth of her being and make her feel truly alive. In those days she just existed. Yet even now that she was fulfilled, her demanding nature was beginning to assert itself. Maybe it was because Alex was with the other two members of the band working on some new songs and she was alone in their new home, and it childishly upset her that he appreciated it so casually. She wondered if he realized that her soul had gone into everything, that he was walking into the space of her heart when he stepped through the door, furnished like her mind with beautiful concepts about reality for him. Her love for Alex was her reason for living, and this sometimes inspired fits of feminist rage in her, because she knew with a man it could never be so. For him love was part of life, not all of it, and she smiled a little thinking how this psychological reality was even manifest in their physiology.

*A woman's sex is inside her, and that's how it is with her love of man, it is her, it's not a part of her life like a man's sex is outside of him, so that he can literally study the situation and get a grip on it. A woman can only feel it; it remains a mystery. Even if she possesses a luminously conscious mind, a part of her is always in the dark and comes alive only with his presence, the wet darkness of the cosmos needing the force of his spirit to be stimulated into the creation of worlds. He fills me and I surround him.*

She sighed. She was constantly thinking deep thoughts when he wasn't around, in touch with his essence even when his body wasn't present for her caresses.

She strolled from the oceanic cave of her bathroom over to the sublime comfort of her violet seashell bed, crawling over the feather mattress just to enjoy its softness, her soul basking like a contentedly bathing cat in the good use they had already put it to. But after a few moments of this indulgence she felt herself becoming inexplicably angry. Yet it was not an unpleasant sensation, so she knelt comfortably on the bed and inwardly observed it.

Everything in the room was shining almost supernaturally – the edges of the dresser, the corner of the clear walls – they were as sharp as knives to the soul's conscious confinement. It wasn't anger; it was the sense of her own unbound energy always welling up inside her with the desire to know itself, this fact becoming a restless frustration of her body without him. Only when he was with her did she know what she was – the pulse of a single heart.

'Oh, Jesus! Why can't I just be mindlessly happy for one evening?'

She leapt off the bed. 'I think I'll have a snack and watch some TV,' she informed the walls of her hallway on which she had hung her paintings. But she paused at one of them with the adventurous sense of being on a spaceship with a world floating by a porthole as she walked past it. 'Life is endlessly exciting if you make it so!' she exclaimed. 'That's it, so why keep conceptualizing? It only gives my psyche a headache. I've got to transcend all this metaphysical stuff and rest silently and happily in Alex's arms. All this thinking is ultimately a form of spirit- clipping if it doesn't stop somewhere! It's a residue of prudery and insecurity!' she proclaimed to her living room. 'All this think, think, thinking, tick, tick, ticking! I just want to explode into endless creativity!' She twirled around in her long white nightgown. 'I'll make him pay for staying away so long and leaving me to pine away in the maze of my brain!'

She ran back into the bedroom, TV and snack forgotten. She removed her nightgown and then strolled back out into her living room, this time not noticing her paintings because she was too into herself. And who this self was was the eternal, adventurous unknown. Her only real steady identity was the one that was aware of her own mystery, the rest of her was a host of unknown selves a clamoring to be heard over the responsible, rational voice of her mind. These selves were pure qualities, not other identities, and tonight she was a killer. She wanted him to become angry at her power over him and beat against her so that she could both surrender to him and fight him with the violence of her response. This was what she wanted tonight, for him to treat her like the passionate strangers they eternally were. Because no matter how much they talked, how well they got to know each other emotionally and physically, his being was an inexhaustible unknown.

She would reduce him to a state of primeval helplessness, the sweet sea foam of his head floating on the waves of ecstasy as in the beginnings of life, her womb the ocean holding him, his sex containing all of him. She wanted to feel the fiery divinity of his spirit that first sparked inert matter to life and set her heart – the sensual core of the world – into motion around him.

She lay back on the couch and waited...

She was lying at the bottom of the sea, the water flowing deliciously warm and heavy over her womb and thighs. Then she felt a strong current slowly pulling on her and she didn't see any reason to resist it. She let her thighs part with the invisible desire of the tide. She gazed at her legs floating over her, admiring their slenderness and enjoying their weightlessness. Suddenly a little fish nudged her opening curiously, as if her pussy was a cave where it could seek refuge from sharks and other predators. She felt it trying to wriggle into her and she moaned with pleasure at its urgency, expecting to feel it slip inside her. But it didn't, it seemed to become caught, and its struggle selfishly filled her with a joy that became deeper and deeper so that she hoped it would remain trapped between her legs forever. But then abruptly it freed itself and she felt something loom over her. *Oh, my God, it must have sensed a shark!* she thought, panicked, and abruptly surfaced from the dream.

Alex was kneeling naked on the couch with her legs in his hands, and his smile did indeed evoke the dangerous sharpness of a shark's fin. 'Turn around.' He lowered her legs and she obeyed him. She bent her arms beneath her head, closing her eyes again and moaning as he parted the lips of her sex with his fingers and slowly filled her with his cock. He put all his weight on top of her and her pussy throbbed with sensations beneath his penetrations. He fell on top of her. 'I love you!' he whispered in her ear, and the more helplessly she moaned the more passionately he assured her of his devotion.

'Alex, lets go over to the chair,' she suggested, eager to give him what he wanted, and he helped her up quickly.

She led him over to the bird chair with its gently arched back and seat. She sat on it sideways, and then lifted her legs up over the back. He pulled her up by the ankles so that only her head rested on the seat then stood over her as she perched her ankles on his shoulders. He gripped her wrists and her hands fluttered beneath the sweet shock of his descent like wings. Standing over her like this he sank fully into her body, his erection plunging deeper and deeper into her wide open sex.

They enjoyed the bird chair for a while then stood in the middle of the living room. She licked his nipples, flicking them lightly with her tongue, and spoke to him silently. 'I will never be tired of you!' She fell to her knees, caressing his body with her cheek. She lifted his penis and kissed him underneath it. She fingered his head delicately as she licked his shaft. 'I want to give you everything because that's what makes me happy!' She rested his stiff length between her breasts and caressed it. 'You are the only one in my mind!' She made a ring with her thumb and finger around his head and moved it up and down quickly, holding his erection firmly at the base with her other hand. 'This is where we are now and it's wonderful here in the flesh...' She concentrated the motion of her thumb and her fingers' living ring in the sensitive area just below his head. Then she let go of him and sat on the carpet a slight distance from him. She raised her legs and grasped his penis between her two feet where the arches formed a hollow, caressing him like this.

He stared down at what was happening for a moment before taking hold of her feet and moving them up and down his rampant cock with passionate curiosity, their blood pulsing through their bodies in rhythm with the music, its melody the loving contact of their eyes as they played on their physical instruments. They almost always made love to music.

The disk ended in perfect time with the enjoyment of this position as she lowered her legs. No experience transcended for her the joy of making love with him to music heightening, deepening, and sustaining the ecstasy so that it achieved impossible dimensions.

Next she lay back on the carpet with him kneeling over her, the tops of his feet resting on the black couch so that he sank all the way inside her again, his penetrating stare devastating her as much or even more than his thrusts. The way he looked at her opened her up so profoundly ecstasy rose like a floodtide inside her, her soft cries mingling with his deep groans. She wanted to tell him how much she loved him, but she couldn't speak, and this gave a painful edge to the pleasure. Even as she was expressing her devotion to him with her trusting submission, she felt that not in all the lifetimes left to the earth before the sun exploded could she convey the depth of her love to him.

Later that same night they were standing in the kitchen having a snack.

'Alex, I don't think I'm going to live very long.'

'What?' He laughed, slipping his free arm around her. 'You're healthy as a panther, Elizabeth.'

'That's just it, I love you too much and it's going to burn me out sooner than everyone who loves less intensely.'

'Then I don't have long to go either, do I?' He kissed her, and then kept eating light-heartedly.

'With a man it's different.'

'Oh, is it?' He raised an eyebrow, only half listening; the other half of him thoroughly enjoying his snack.

'Yes and our different attitudes at this moment proves my point. Every time we come together I find it harder to separate myself from you, but you're not at all phased.'

He finished his sandwich, brushed his hands free of crumbs, then suddenly swept her up into his arms. 'Elizabeth, you have to get out of your Greek Tragedy mode.' He carried her though the living room. 'Life is the joy of polarity, not the sorrow of contradiction.'

'Oh, God, Alex, I worship you, you're so right.'

He lay her gently down on the bed. 'You see, I think about things too. I know how much you feel for me, you don't have to be afraid that I don't know, that I don't understand you or believe you. But I can't talk to you the way Mike does and the way Jim did, that's not how I'm made. You just have to trust me and know that when I say "I love you" I mean all those deep thoughts you're thinking.'

She closed her eyes. 'Oh, Alex! I have this disease of conceptualization, but you're curing me of it.' She grasped his hand. 'You're burning it out of me with your presence… but it takes time, because for so long I was afraid and unfulfilled and it was all that kept me alive. I'm…' But she couldn't finish because he was soothing her with a kiss.

'My presence?' He smiled.

# Chapter Nine

Elizabeth was discovering something that surprised her, and at first she thought it should upset her, until she realized that what she actually felt was a wonderfully growing peace. She was not possessed by the need to make passionate love to Alex all the time. She found that the memory of a long, intense session was just as fulfilling to her. The evening after they made such good use of their living room, she was content to rest in his arms and gaze into his eyes remembering all his expressions, caresses and gestures as if they were happening then. Except that the intense fire of the union was dimmed enough that she could consciously gaze at its beauty and let it warm her soul, her love for him transcending the physical devastation and inspiring in her a profound certainty of the divine nature of life.

At first she had found it almost impossibly difficult to deal with the days when he watched baseball or engaged in other, for her, similarly mundane activities.

*How can he be so intense and yet so normal?* Was all she could think. But even then, deep down, she knew it was her problem that she felt this way, and she began to work it out with herself. What she could not accept were the limits of mortality; she possessed an other-worldly sort of restlessness that did not go away even when she was fulfilled in every respect. So much so that she began to look forward to Alex's next tour, missing the orgasmic activity and exhaustion of road life. Looking back on it she only remembered its burning intensity – dancing in the cosmically dark wings, making love to him in atmospheric rooms that floated like different worlds through the darkness of her memory. What Elizabeth wanted was to live in the powerfully unconditional realm of art all the time; she resented the inertness of daily life. But doing things for Alex brought a joy even to the smallest, most routine actions, permeating every moment of her day like the sun so that nothing felt mundane. Her tastes did not change, and she still did not want children, even though she knew they could probably teach her a lot about herself.

As a little girl she had been fascinated by the few movies she had seen where a woman danced in front of men for their pleasure. Salome was the most famous, and she had always resented the infamous character attached to all such dancers as a result, unable to understand the split between the dark, witchy woman and the virtuous wife. This classic division had always tormented her because she knew she was both and could no more choose between them than she could prefer one beat of her heart to another. And the official replacement, the feminist woman, had not helped in the least. At fifteen, she had been unconsciously terrified that there was no man left on earth worthy of a dancing witch with a heart of gold like herself, powerfully sensual, spiritually virtuous, and consciously independent all in one. Her emotional experience of things was sacred and therefore to the modern mentality, exaggerated. But she had always been how she was, and now she was taking private dance classes with a young man she had met at a party she and Alex attended. Albert needed extra money and was overjoyed to earn it by helping her choreography some songs. He came over first thing in the morning and they worked for three to four hours in a spare room in the basement adjoining Alex's personal recording studio. She promptly converted it into a dance studio, installing an exercise bar and wall-to-wall mirrors, the wooden floor already provided.

She kissed Alex's lips, leaving him peacefully in their violet seashell bed, put on her dance gear – assorted colors of tights and shimmering bodices – drank down a glass of orange juice, and ran down to the studio to warm up a little before Albert arrived.

\* \* \*

'Elizabeth, I know what you want, but the body has its limits, and you have to learn to work with them.' Albert was happily exasperated with her. 'You can't follow all the instruments at once!'

'I know that, but I'm not doing enough!'

'All right, listen to me, try this… Your arms follow the sweeping range of the guitar like this… while you run in time with the drums…'

'And the singer's voice twirls me around with what he's saying…'

'Very nice! But you're going to have to put pauses in the choreography to allow for your corporeality,' he teased, smiling.

'Nonsense! I *am* the music,' she teased back.

'No way, you don't sweat enough, and you're still not sufficiently limber. You have to work at the bar a lot more.'

'I know, but I hate it.' She walked over to the CD player and switched it off.

'You can't be a dancer without it, Elizabeth.'

She pinned up loose hairs coiling down her neck and shoulders like mischievously straying snakes. 'I don't want to be a dancer; I just want to dance for Alex. I'm sure Salome didn't slave over a bar.'

'If I was you, I'd take dancing seriously.'

'I do take it seriously, Albert, I want to dance for Alex!'

'I meant professionally.'

'I thought you wanted me to take it seriously.'

'Forget it.'

'There are plenty of stunningly athletic, talented dancers out there to entertain audiences. I'm interested in a more intimate expression… an extension of love-making, not theatre.

The subtlety I seek would be lost on the stage, it's meant for the dimensions of a room embracing the movements like a lover, so that the person watching really feels it... Because his presence is what the choreography is all about...'

'Shut-up and stretch.' He shoved her towards the bar.

'All right, don't be so pushy!' She laughed, pleased at his rough impatience.

Alex appeared in the doorway in his black house shorts, brushing his hair out of his face and smiling at her sleepily.

She ran over to him, flinging her arms around his neck and lifting one of her legs behind her as she gracefully fell against him. 'Good morning!'

They smiled into each other's eyes, and then he unwrapped her arms from around him. 'How's she doing?' he asked Albert.

'If she stretched as much as she philosophizes, she'd be another Isadora Duncan.'

'Did you hear that?' Alex shoved her away. 'Stretch!'

'Yes, master.'

'I want her to suffer, Albert, do you hear me?'

'I sure do.'

\* \* \*

One evening Alex was out and Elizabeth was tipsy on half a bottle of Chardonnay. She took two candles into the dance studio, lighting them and placing them on opposite sides of the room, then she ran back into the bedroom and stripped. She glanced at her jewel box, smiled to herself, and carried it back into the studio. She set it down in a corner by the CD player, sank down onto her hands and knees, and looked at her reflection as cautiously as if it was a panther about to leap out at her. The sight of her naked body gripped her vision like fangs, and she grew deeply relaxed beneath the mysteriously hungry weight of her own beauty. She remained crouching before her reflection, her dark hair coiling over her delicate breasts and slender arms, her eyes perfectly black in the low light – the star-filled darkness of the universe staring at itself. She crawled towards her image, thinking, *I could eat him alive! The only reason I don't is because I'd miss him so much!*

She smiled, rising, and turned on the CD player. She quickly searched her jewel box, slipping beaten gold bracelets all the way up her arms and around her ankles. That was all she wanted to wear.

She twirled to the center of the dance floor, partnered by shadows from the flickering candle flames. She dutifully stretched a little on the bar, the boredom of the routine alleviated by the pleasure of watching herself doing it naked in the hauntingly lit space.

The song was ending and the one she wanted was about to come on so she positioned herself in the center of the floor. She wanted to get it right and thoroughly feel it and enjoy it at the same time. *That's the trick in life as in the dance, control and flow, conceptual choreography and the rhythmic pleasure of day-to-day.*

Silence, and her body paused in the center of the room suffused with candlelight reflecting universes in the mirrors and gleaming in the gold around her arms and legs.

\* \* \*

After dancing she lay sprawled across the floor. Her blood, her life, felt so hot and sweet in those moments like a divine candle burning down the wick of her spinal chord. She was turning to rest on her back when she suddenly saw Alex silhouetted in the doorway. The shock of his sudden presence was like a penetration and she lay perfectly motionless beneath the weight of his awareness of her, her arms straight above her head, one of her legs gently bent.

He was dressed all in black, his form hauntingly emerging from the darkness for her to see and feel, the candles standing elegantly by like the sentinels of this mystery. It was almost painful the happiness she felt in his presence, and the experience of his features masked by shadows weakened her so profoundly she lay utterly motionless and submissive as he approached her.

'Are you going to dance for me?' he asked quietly.

'No, not tonight, master.'

'If you were really my slave, you would have to do whatever I wanted whenever I wanted.'

'Theoretically, yes.'

'Then dance for me now.' He loomed over her.

'No, you dance...' She raised her leg and caressed his thigh with her bare foot. 'Dance in me...'

He held her leg up by the heel and admired the beaten-gold ankle bracelet. He passed his hand up and down her calf slowly, contemplatively. 'I want to see you dance.'

'You will, master, soon, I have a wondrous ancient evening planned.'

'Let's do it now.'

'No.' She was resisting him in the hope that he would somehow force her to do his bidding. *But that isn't his way*, she thought, gratefully offering him her other leg. He took it and spread them open so he could stare down into the shadowy depths between them. 'Come in...' she coaxed him.

'I don't know, it's pretty dark and slippery down there, it doesn't seem like a safe path to take.'

'But it leads straight to paradise, I promise.'

'Are you sure?'

'Positive.'

'I don't know, my mother told me never to listen to girls like you.'

'Like me?'

'Yes, the kind that lie naked in the middle of candlelit dance floors with their legs spread open invitingly.' He smiled, pushing her legs back, and she let them fall straight over her head so her toes touched the floor behind her.

'Now look what you've done,' she complained. 'You've bent me all out of shape.'

"Mm, yes, but this is a much more functional form..."

# Chapter Ten

'Okay, my sweet little oyster, where are we going tonight?' Alex cradled her beneath his arm where they were sitting up in their violet seashell.

'Egypt when I was eighteen,' she replied at once. 'I went there alone. I made my father promise that would be my high school graduation present, so the day I was supposed to be wearing a silly cap and gown, I was on a plane to Cairo. I stayed with an American family stationed there, so I was on my own most of the time, not with some stupid tourist group. The first place I went was Alexandria by the sea, the city of the Ptolemy's, built late in Egypt's history, where Cleopatra ruled. You should see how at night the streets come to life. The weather is ideal, and the air is still charged with vibrations left over from passionate ancient festivals. I took a carriage ride by myself while the Kelly's waited for me back at the hotel. It was an open-air black coach with a brown horse, and apparently the coachman wasn't well trained in where to take a tourist because we went through the seething heart of Alexandria instead of sticking to the polished fringes...'

'And that's where I come in, when you're all alone in a carriage in the dark heart of corrupt Alexandria, far, far away from the respectable American couple protecting you.'

'That's it, because during the long carriage ride we passed a car surrounded by Arabs, and in the middle of the group, leaning against it, was a blonde man lifting a cigarette to his lips as I passed, and our eyes met. I tried to look back at him, but the black canopy of the carriage was in the way, and for years after that I was sure I had seen and lost my soul mate that night in Alexandria.'

'But he wasn't your soul mate, you were actually spared–'

'Don't tell me!'

'Okay, let's go.'

'Let's go.'

She got up, turned the Dream Recorder on, and moved the black color knob until the walls of the room were a deep, haunting blue evoking the waters of the Mediterranean at night, the ceiling above them always black and glimmering with glow-in-the-dark stars, the way the night sky looks when not contaminated by light pollution. Then she cuddled back in his arms, smiling into his eyes for a moment as the mist of the screen and their combined imaginations became a visible world. This more expensive Dream Recorder picked up daydreams as well as sleeping dreams and possessed two channels for combined experiences with another psyche. The setting was formed by the visualization of the two dreamers, and the action was like life – their reaction to each other, each of them appearing as they pictured themselves.

They usually talked and laughed softly as the action unfolded, and the images on the large screen were indefinitely suspended whenever they stopped concentrating on the action, because this dissipated the flow of energy to the machine. But if they began kissing and caressing, the dream would continue unfolding since they were aroused by its plot and images. Thus laughter and small talk acted like an omniscient god and froze the action whenever they pleased, but desire perpetuated and intensified it.

'There you are,' Alex whispered.

A black, horse-drawn carriage was making its way down a

dark, narrow street flanked by old, run-down buildings and open-air cafes where Arabs in traditional dress sat playing dominoes and drawing on water pipes. The full moon remained parallel with her carriage as if when she stepped out its enchanted silver path was the one she was going to follow.

'You're just up ahead,' she informed Alex. 'There, see that gathering of Western-clad Arabs? You're in the center of them like a luminous god surrounded by your dark apostles...'

'A luminous god, huh? You've got something coming to you.'

'Oh, good!'

'Okay, shut-up and get in character.'

'I am.'

'No you're not, you're eighteen and perfectly innocent. Were you?' He looked at her and the carriage stopped moving.

'Yes, I was, I didn't lose my virginity until I was nineteen, if you can believe it.'

'Good.'

They stared back at the screen and the carriage proceeded on its way. Alex was lifting a cigarette to his lips, his golden hair waving softly down to his shoulders in the style he had worn years ago, his blue eyes harder, narrow with the self-centered intensity of youth; wolf-like in the direct, hungry way they fell on her as she passed. He was all in black, but his shirt was half open, exposing his pale skin. She was wearing a brown skirt and sleeveless shirt, her full dark hair only as long as his, her long legs beautifully sun-browned. Their eyes met, his gray-blue electric gaze penetrating the deep, virginal soil of her brown irises. An image flashed briefly moved on the screen – the inside of her skirt staining with blood as he tore it open in front and penetrated her.

'You fiend!' Elizabeth whispered. 'All you want is to deflower me and toss me away, and here I am thinking you're my soul mate!'

'Ssssh!'

The carriage was moving on and she was looking back desperately. Then there was a loud commotion and her driver glanced around him, surprised, as he was surrounded and the horses forced to a stop by the men that had been lounging around the car. Elizabeth sat frozen with terror and joy because she knew the blonde man had commanded them to stop her. He rose up into the carriage with her, throwing out his cigarette butt, and she felt her heart fly into the night with it, burning with all her dreams, the innocent intensity of her youth already lost as he gazed at her with his cool blue wolf's eyes.

'Hello.' He smiled. 'Would you mind if I rode with you?'

'No…' She looked away from him as the carriage started moving again.

'What's your name?' he asked gently, putting a firm finger beneath her chin and making her look at him again.

'Elizabeth!' she exhaled as if it were her last breath, and he confirmed this feeling by kissing her suddenly, his tongue roguishly introducing itself to hers. She drew back, sliding away from him on the seat.

'I'm sorry, I should have told you my name first. Alex.' He pulled her to him, holding her firmly and kissing her again.

'Let me go!' she cried, but not loud enough to catch her driver's attention.

'Don't be afraid,' he whispered, resting his lips more politely on her cheek a moment. 'It's just that you're so beautiful, I can't help myself. Cleopatra couldn't hold a candle to you, I

swear it. You look just like an ancient Egyptian queen, Elizabeth…'

She mysteriously relaxed as he shifted the blame to her, making her feel this was happening because she secretly wanted it to, and that if she stopped desiring it his behavior would change accordingly.

'Where are you going?' he asked nicely, and she was torn between the need to verbally answer him and the urge to silently respond to his hand wandering over her breasts and down towards her skirt.

'I'm going back to the hotel... the Kelly's are expecting me...'

'Who are they?' He gazed down at her and she couldn't answer him because the Kelly's had nothing to do with what her body was experiencing now. His hands were making her feel fearlessly alive. 'Forget about them...' He slowly pushed her skirt up the brown warmth of her thighs and rested his hand gently between them, his thumb idly caressing the soft inner flesh near her sex. 'Stay with me... Don't worry, you can take me to meet them later, just stay with me for a while and I'll show you what ancient Egypt was really like...' He was whispering in her ear and her body, with a will of its own, slipped a little lower in the seat so that his hand came to rest directly between her legs. 'That's it, don't be afraid...' His firm, warm palm rubbed against the soft, smooth layer of her panties and her awareness became disconnected, spark-like thoughts convincing her that staying with him was right.

'But people are looking...' she protested half-heartedly.

'That's true.' He lowered her skirt again gently. 'We'll go somewhere.' He yelled something to the driver in Arabic.

'Where?' Now that he wasn't touching her, she was afraid again. 'They'll be worried about me. They'll think something terrible happened to me...' But he stared at her in such a way that she couldn't concentrate on the abstraction of this fretting American couple. His eyes and his hands were suddenly the only real things in the universe. Returning to the Kelly's seemed like choosing the dimensions of a postcard over reality.

All Elizabeth could see walking up the narrow wooden stairway of the building he took her to was his blonde hair, so reassuringly soft and luminous in the unconscious darkness of her fear, his firm arm around her a justification for her uncertainty, his embrace holding her together when otherwise she felt she would have disintegrated with terror. Yet he was the cause of this quivering point of fear lodged like a sweetly poisoned arrow between her legs. The experience was sacred in its overpowering quality, but then they reached a door and it was like a slap waking her from the roman-

## Moonlit Dreams

tic dream of the ascent – a wooden slab on which she supernaturally saw the corpse of her romantic dreams lying. She tried to pull away from him, but he held her firmly.

'No...' she protested, and pulling away from him started running down the stairs, Mrs. Kelly's dyed blonde head like a safe beacon in the darkness before her.

'Elizabeth!' His hurt, desperate tone was such a surprise it arrested her flight more successfully than his hands, which grasped her arms a second later. 'I thought you weren't afraid any more,' he whispered.

'But I am!' she breathed, pleading for his comfort.

'There's nothing to be afraid of, Elizabeth, I'm not going to hurt you, I'm going to make you feel good, and there's nothing wrong with that, trust me...'

'But I just met you... I don't even know you...'

'You will soon. You'll know everything about me and you won't be afraid, you'll beg for more...' Still standing behind her he caressed her breasts with a controlled violence, and the motion of his hands was like the slow music used to rouse a dormant snake she felt uncoiling between her legs and rising through her body up to his hands, her nipples becoming burning red tongues desperate to taste his flesh against hers.

'She's giving in too easily,' Alex murmured in her ear, beginning to feel her breasts along with his dream self.

'But she can't help it you're so irresistible, so persuasive... oh, yes...'

'Don't forget you're a virgin...'

'Oh, no, I won't forget ...'

'It's supposed to hurt...'

'Oh, God, yes, it's killing me... but wait, they're not even in the room... stop! They can't do it on the stairs!'

'Oh, yes they can!'

'No, stop!'

'Don't be afraid...'

'I don't want them to do it there!'

'Yes, you do…'
'No!'
'Yes… yes… yes!'
'Oh, God… oh, Alex…'
'I'm not God.'
'Yes you are…'

In the dream her virginal blood was staining one of the steps beneath the relentless force of his thrusts. She was crying, whimpering, certain she could not bear what he was doing to her one more second, until his warm lips covered hers and parted in a kiss.

'Talk to me, be nice to me, say something, I'm a virgin!'
'I am being nice to you!'
'Tell me you love me!'
'I love you, you're beautiful, you feel so good… tell me how much you like it.'
'Oh, God, I love it, don't stop…'
'Beg for more.'
'Oh, please, don't stop, please, not ever!'

He groaned, coming inside her on the bed and on the screen, and then their shared fantasy slowly faded out, becoming a hazy white cloud of light as if their characters ascended to heaven on the climax, a smile rising through the body of their lips as they gazed at the creative spirit in each other's eyes.

**Coming in the Summer of 2005
from Magic Carpet Books...**

# Guilty Pleasures

**By
Maria Isabel Pita**

Guilty Pleasures explores the passionate willingness of women throughout the ages to offer themselves up to the forces of love. Historical facts are seamlessly woven into intensely graphic sexual encounters beginning with ancient Egypt and journeying down through the centuries to the present and beyond.

Beneath the covers of Guilty Pleasures you'll find over twenty erotic love stories with a profound feel for the times and places where they occur. An ancient Egyptian priestess... a courtesan rising to fame in Athen's Golden Age... the lovely sacrifice of a Druid rite... a Romanian Count's wicked mistress... and many more are all one eternal woman in Guilty Pleasures.

Turn the page for an exciting excerpt...

## Covenant Transport
## Dorchester, Massachusetts 1933

Six days a week at four o'clock in the morning, Elizabeth Reed drops her brother off at the bakery, and then heads home again for a few more hours sleep. Rising before the sun depresses her; it mysteriously robs her of her sense of direction and she knows where she is going only in the most literal sense. During the relatively short drive traffic signals flash yellow suns over the empty black space of the roads. One morning it rains gently on her way home and a rising fog imbues the streetlamps with a ghostly aura. Hers is the only car in sight except for a truck pulling up to the curb on the opposite side of the street. Its multiple headlights are shaped like a cross around which the mist flows in restless sheets. Two words are written in white letters across the truck's dark body: COVENANT TRANSPORT.

\* \* \*

Three mornings later, Elizabeth passes the truck again. An abundance of stars are visible above the empty office buildings as she catches sight of the driver jumping lightly down from behind the wheel. He is strikingly tall and his silhouette in a long black coat flows like a solid shadow in front of the headlights' luminous cross.

\*\*\*

The struggling ad company where she works as an invoice typist finally goes under, forcing her to look for another job like so many others, and Sunday she begins the dreary search through the meager classifieds.

On Monday she answers an obscure little ad for a receptionist that feels in keeping with her brief resume. She suffers a strangely pleasant shock when she drives to the address, 1048 Elder Street, the numbers visible now without the truck parked in front of them. Elizabeth is somehow certain the job is meant for her. She considers 'coincidence' a dirty word; she has always imagined she senses invisible forces working around her, perhaps because it's inconceivable to her that her unique beauty is only a random combination of chemicals.

Stepping out of the old Ford Model-T her brother manages to keep running, she glances down at her faint reflection in the driver's window. She has recently sacrificed most of her long hair to the indifferent altar of a salon floor. Like cupped hands, two neat black curves now offer her face to the world, the trim bangs combined with her full mouth giving her a seductive look. It's the latest fashion and in keeping with the independent spirit she exhibited since birth, to her late mother's chagrin.

There is no sign beneath the black metal numbers on the heavy wooden door, and the large front room she steps into is empty. No paintings hang on the stark white walls, no furniture breaks up the polished gleam of the wooden floor, and the ceiling is an unfinished web of black beams rising much higher above her than she would have thought possible from the building's facade. The space is dimly lit by sunlight filtering in through the opaque glass of two windows flanking the door, and by a brass lamp sitting on a small desk she suddenly notices tucked into a corner.

'Good afternoon,' she says to the blonde woman seated

behind it. 'My name is Elizabeth Reed. I've come to apply for the position advertised in the paper.'

'Good afternoon, Elizabeth.' The woman rises from behind the desk. 'Come this way, please.'

A natural blonde judging by her complexion, the current receptionist is as tall and beautiful as Ginger Rogers. She leads Elizabeth into a narrow corridor faintly lit by a naked light bulb where she opens a door and smiles her into the room beyond. Then the door clicks shut behind her, leaving her alone with a monstrously large desk and the figure draped in black seated behind it.

'Good afternoon, dear,' the nun says, her smile weary. 'Please, have a seat.'

Elizabeth perches on the wooden chair facing the paper-strewn surface.

'You are the ninth girl I have seen today, Elizabeth,' the nameless sister states sadly, her watery green eyes framed by a delta of wrinkles. 'Not one of them was right for the position.'

'Oh...' Elizabeth has no idea what else to say as she produces her painstakingly typed resume.

The old woman accepts it and studies it for a moment, her thin lips pursed. 'Mm... very good, and now you are here.'

Elizabeth takes advantage of the opening. 'Where is here exactly, Sister?'

'Forgive me, my dear, I thought you knew where you were. This is an annex of St. John's Church. Primarily it serves as a storage facility, but a kitchen in the back is where volunteers bake the Host on Saturdays. We store all charitable donations of food and clothing here. You met Candy. She answers phone calls and accepts gifts during the day, but we also need someone to be here at night, because God's servants never rest, you know.'

'Oh, I know, I've been driving my brother to a bakery every morning at four a.m. and I've seen one of your trucks.'

'Oh, excellent.' A childish grin smoothes away her wrinkles

before vanishing like a mirage in a cracked desert. 'Candy will give you the appropriate forms to fill out. I trust ten dollars a week is acceptable?'

'Oh, yes, thank you, Sister!'

'We need you to begin tonight, Elizabeth. I will give you the key. Your hours are midnight to nine, Monday through Friday. The women who do the baking only come in on Saturdays, so you will not have to deal with them. The young man who handles our deliveries will introduce himself. We're expecting new cushions for the pews tonight at around four a.m.'

The tall, dark figure in the long black coat... the thought of him more than the generous pay makes this graveyard shift feel potentially intriguing instead of mind-numbingly dull.

\* \* \*

Elizabeth is back in the echoing front room seated behind the desk with the brass lamp and its green glass shade. She is wearing a long-sleeved black dress with a lace-trimmed collar that buttons down the front, and the pearl-drop earrings her grandmother left her, her most treasured possession.

She let herself into the office at six minutes to midnight according to the black-and-white clock hanging over her head now. The absolute darkness and silence intimidated her, and she still cannot quite shake off a subtle feeling of anxiety.

Except for a trip to a closet-sized bathroom, she has been sitting in the surprisingly comfortable desk chair for two hours reading. The first thing she did was explore the slightly warped drawers, but she found nothing of interest, only the usual pens and pencils, paper clips, loose staples and writing pads.

She tries to keep her attention buried in the plot of her book, but boredom is sucking the energy out of her drop by drop, second by second, and she doesn't know how she can possibly stay awake all night.

Standing up to get blood flowing through her stiff muscles,

she walks over to one of the windows beside the door and flips open the dusty blinds. If she can wait another two hours for the driver to show up she can just as easily survive two centuries. Her only companion in this silent vigil is the streetlight on the corner. The way the top of the lamp post curves over the black asphalt evokes a person with his head lowered in grief, yet even through the walls of the building she senses the subliminal hum of the power flowing through it.

Headlights abruptly cut through her thoughts as a truck pulls up outside and the words COVENANT TRANSPORT fill her vision.

She opens the door and steps out into the cold darkness just in time to see the driver walk out of the headlights' luminous stream. He is concentrating on the clipboard in his hand, but he looks up instantly in response to the sound of her high-heels on the sidewalk.

For once reality outdoes her imagination; he is so intensely handsome her voice seems to slip on his features and all she can manage is a breathless, 'Good evening!' Hugging herself, she hurries back inside, and retreats all the way behind the desk.

He follows her. 'Good morning,' he corrects her, setting his clipboard down in front of her. 'My name is John.' His voice is deep and quiet.

'Pleased to meet you, John, I'm Elizabeth.'

'You are beautiful, Elizabeth.'

The direct compliment literally takes her breath away. 'Thank you...'

'How many men have had the pleasure of using your lovely body, Elizabeth?'

'What?' she gasps. 'It is none—'

'Do not tell me it is none of my business, Elizabeth, because you would be lying.'

'I may have bobbed my hair, sir, but I'm a respectable woman and a very particular one.' Naturally she has allowed a handful of men to make love to her, but they all disappointed her in the end for one reason or another; however, that doesn't make her a tramp. 'I still subscribe to the old-fashioned belief that there's someone special out there I'm meant to be with, and until such time as-'

'Do you really believe that, Elizabeth?'

'Yes,' she replies fervently, transfixed by the ideal symmetry of his features. Despite the freezing temperatures outside there is not the slightest hint of color in his cheeks.

He turns away abruptly with a cape-like flourish of his coat and leaves the front door open behind him, letting in the cold.

Even though he just raped her sensibilities by asking her such an intimate question, his perfect bone structure and proud carriage make it impossible for her to resent him. She remains rooted to the desk chair thoughtlessly awaiting his return, shivering.

A minute later she watches him wheel in what looks very much like a narrow wooden coffin.

'I assume those are new cushions for the pews,' she remarks. Daring to venture out from behind the desk again, she follows him down the long corridor to a door at the end. 'Let me,' she offers to open it for him and the knob turns so easily she nearly stumbles into the pitch-black space. Moving lithely out of his way, she searches the wall for a light switch as the darkness swallows him and his burden. At last she finds the switch and flicks it up, but nothing happens.

'Don't bother.' He reappears dragging the empty two-wheeler behind him. 'It's dead.'

She does not want to act like a puppy trotting at his heels, so she sits back down at the desk as he returns to the truck.

His next trip to the storage room is made in a silence punctuated by a long, penetrating look as he passes her desk. 'Well, Elizabeth,' he says on his way back out again, 'do you think you will like your new position?'

'That all depends, John. How long have you been doing this?'

'Doing what, flirting with beautiful women or driving a truck?'

'And I'm sure you could easily fill that truck with all your conquests,' she retorts.

'Naturally,' he pauses beside her, 'but that does not mean I am easy to please. A girl like you should not be alone all night, Elizabeth. Or do you enjoy being awake while most everyone is asleep?' He glances around them. 'Can you feel all their dreams flying through the air like spirits? It is so much easier to come up with interesting ideas at night, ideas too subtle to be born when everyone's mind is awake and tuned into rational fears and concerns.' He holds her eyes. 'If you know what I mean, Elizabeth.'

'Oh, yes, I do. I've been driving my brother to a bakery every morning at four o'clock and the atmosphere is different at that hour, and not just because it's dark... I've seen your truck parked out in the mist...'

He perches on the edge of the desk, looming over her in his black coat. 'Do you believe in an afterlife, Elizabeth?' he asks quietly, gazing steadily into her eyes.

'Yes, but I don't believe it's something that just happens to us,' she answers thoughtfully, intrigued by the unusual conversation. 'I believe there are as many different afterlives as there are people. I mean, unless you develop your spiritual senses in this life you'll probably have a pretty scary experience. Death isn't just one big black empty space we all vanish into, and I don't believe it's a perfect ready-made heaven, either. To believe that is like being a baby in the womb imagining life after birth as either a featureless void or a carefree paradise.' Sharing these profound thoughts with him excites her so much she forgets to feel shy. 'I think dying must be like another birth, except that everything gets turned inside out and your inner world manifests around you.'

'I have some free time,' he says quietly. 'Will you share a cup of tea with me in the back, Elizabeth?'

\*\*\*

The cavernous kitchen is dominated by a long wooden table worn shiny smooth from years of pounding and kneading the body of Christ. It is flanked by rows of ovens, and the fact that half the overhead lights are dead makes the room feel strangely morgue-like. It is dark in the corner where a decrepit little gas stove adjoins a large porcelain sink. She seats herself at the small wooden table in front of the stove while John starts some water boiling in the kettle, his back to her. Except for the occasional white flash of his hands he is three different degrees of darkness from his black hair to his coat down to his leather boots.

'I like your ideas, Elizabeth.' He sets a chipped tea cup in front of her and seats himself opposite her.

'Thank you, John.'

He crosses his arms over his chest and his intensely serious expression makes him almost too handsome to look at. 'Are you pleased to find out everything you believe is true, Elizabeth?'

His choice of tenses confuses her but she ignores it. 'I would have to be dead first, so I think I can wait to find out.'

'You do not have a choice, Elizabeth. Do you really believe in this strange position in the middle of the night doing nothing?'

She smiles to conceal a climax of emotions inside her as she suddenly realizes what he is up to. 'You mean I'm... I'm dead?' She crosses her legs to hide how much it arouses her to think of him as a dark angel.

He continues gazing silently into her eyes.

'I don't know it yet, but I've... I've died,' she goes on, imagining that he's waiting for her to develop the macabre plot, 'and this place is just a metaphor my soul is fashioning around me. And that beautiful receptionist, and the old nun who hired me, are the two aspects of my nature, sensual and spiritual. Also, it's after hours, so everything is dark and silent as the grave.'

'You are very bright, Elizabeth.' His smile is sinister. 'But what does that make me?'

'Either an angel or a devil... yet I hope you can somehow be both.'

'Then they will have to come together inside you, Elizabeth.' Rising abruptly, he walks around the table to her.

Her eyes close from the weakening blow of desire she experiences as he grips her arm and pulls her to her feet. She doesn't resist as he leads her over to the table. He grasps her around the waist and lifts her on to it, and still she doesn't protest as he pushes her dress up far enough to spread her legs and stand between them. His mouth opens over hers, luring her into a warm, fluid realm alive with the rising, rhythmic excitement of flight. His deep kiss is a substantial yet unrestrained dimension in which his controlled force overwhelms her and makes it impossible to think clearly about what is happening. Only vaguely does she wonder if her wantonness will lose her the badly needed ten dollars a week promised to her by a nun who would promptly fire her if she could see her now. He keeps a firm grip on her upper arms even though there's no chance of her getting away, and she's glad his hands don't wander elsewhere as he explores her only through a lingering kiss. Still, she is increasingly afraid... or excited... she can't quite tell the difference. His haunting insinuations opened her up to his advances, but they are not responsible for the languid way her head falls back as he tongues her more deeply than any man ever has. He almost seems to want to suck the breath out of her lungs and her chest heaves from the strain when he at last pulls away.

Gazing into her eyes, he gently grasps her left wrist and draws it up to his lips. He caresses her sleeve up out of his way and kisses the faint blue delta of veins visible through her delicate skin. She watches him with her mouth parted in growing wonder, her eyes shining with a longing she can't put into words. At first the sight of his strong white teeth and well-defined canines is just another aesthetic revelation, just another visible reason to surrender to her attraction to him, but when their surprisingly sharp ends begin sinking into her skin she instinctively struggles to pull her arm free.

'Stop!' she gasps, but he keeps her slender wrist fiercely planted between his lips. Pain rises inside her in a deafening symphony, its fiery director forcing all her senses and perceptions into one climactic sensation as he bites into her flesh growling deep in his throat.

'Oh, my God!' she cries. 'What are you doing? Stop! Please, John, stop! Stop!'

He raises his head.

She can't believe his lips are stained a deep, beautiful red cosmetics can never hope to duplicate. 'You just... you just sucked my blood!' Yet her exclamation isn't completely one of horror; she sounds more like a child whose playmate has exceeded the boundaries of an exciting game by doing something utterly unexpected and shocking, so that her pain is tempered by a thrilled admiration shining in her eyes beneath a resentful veil of tears.

He whispers, 'Have you heard of vampires, Elizabeth?'

'Of course I've heard of vampires, but they don't... they don't really exist...'

'How do you know the undead are only a myth, Elizabeth? How can you be so sure we are not real?'

She stares at her wrist struggling to understand the puncture wounds in her flesh that might have been made by a very large cat as myriads of fears flock into her mind like bats. The vivid red holes are dangerously deep, and looking back up into his silver-gray eyes – into the bottomless black holes of his pupils – she realizes her soul was lost to him from the moment she saw his silhouette take shape against the luminous cross of headlights. The only question is what will happen to her body...

'You are so beautiful, Elizabeth. Your soul is uniquely intoxicating to me, like no other I have ever tasted. I must have you...'

She wants to say, 'This isn't funny anymore, John!' but it never was funny, it was arousing, and it still is somehow even though the stimulating edge of her fear is painfully sharp now.

He lets go of her wrist and steps back. Now is the moment when she should make an effort to get away from him, but she doesn't move. She is transfixed by the way his eyes close as he licks his lips to savor the flavor her of her blood as if earth's most delicious ingredients are concentrated within it. His eyelids are so smooth and white they look carved from marble as he gazes blindly up towards heaven. He isn't looking at her, she could theoretically slip off the table and run from the kitchen, but she still doesn't move, and her passivity is a mystery she is so desperately trying to comprehend she can't think straight; she can't think at all. And then it's too late because his eyes are open again.

'Stand up and take your dress off for me, Elizabeth.'

The indignant exclamation, 'What kind of a girl do you think I am?' flashes through her mind but only like distant lightning; there is no real thunder, no true outrage in it. Her pride and her virtue are still mysteriously intact as she slips down off the edge of the table and begins unbuttoning her dress, an intoxicating blend of fear and desire causing her fingers to tremble forcing her to concentrate on the task. She gazes demurely at the bone-colored buttons of his coat as she slips the dress off her shoulders, hesitating only for a heartbeat before exposing her naked breasts, too young and pert to require the support of a bra.

'Look into my eyes, Elizabeth. I want you to see how beautiful you are.'

She obeys him, and caresses the dress down carefully over

her garters, exposing the soft bush concealing her sex followed by the firm pale flesh of her thighs. A moment later all she is wearing in the middle of a church kitchen are a black garter belt, black stockings and black high-heels.

He is upon her so swiftly she doesn't have time to take a breath to cry out. The cold depths of his coat enfold her slender body as he bends her backwards and clutches her left thigh to lift her leg up against him. A shrill scream echoes through the cavernous kitchen and drowns out her shocked gasp as his teeth easily penetrate the fine skin of her neck. He shifts her weight in his arms in order to get the best possible grip on her, and she clings to his shoulders as if to keep her consciousness from being swept away on a blinding current of pain irresistibly confused with a powerful, erotic undertow… the harder she struggles against the profound sensation the more relentlessly she feels herself carried her away on it… she doesn't have the strength to fight it… suddenly she doesn't understand why she's even resisting something so intensely, breathtakingly pleasurable… she closes her eyes, vaguely aware that only his arms are holding her up as her racing heartbeats begin slowing down, willingly obeying the savoring, sensual rhythm of his throat swallowing her blood in increasingly generous, violently warm mouthfuls…

The kettle stops screaming, and suddenly able to hear herself think she gasps, 'Stop! Oh, my God, please stop!'

His teeth feel like two long and impossibly hard erections pulling reluctantly out of her body. He releases her, and she sinks to her knees as if her black stockings are only ashes or shadows, without substance. She rests her cheek against one of his cold black boots, and its unyielding reality reassures her. When he yanks her back up to her feet, she welcomes his rough handling like the most profound tenderness, and some part of her she can't resist offers the other virginal side of her neck up as a willing sacrifice to his passionate hunger.

'You are mine now, Elizabeth.' He takes her hand and leads

her back down the narrow corridor into the empty front room. 'Sign here,' he commands, handing her his clipboard, 'and release your soul to me.'

She finds a red pen in the desk, and with an unsteady hand signs her full name on the blank white page.

'Look at the clock, Elizabeth.'

She glances up at the black-and-white face. The arms are still at 2:09, the moment she got up to look out the window and saw his truck pull up.

He heads for the door.

'Wait, John!' The last thing she wants in the universe is to be left naked and alone.

'I will be back as soon as you have accepted the truth, Elizabeth,' he promises without looking back, and the door closes silently behind him.

Standing at the window, she listens to the rumble of the truck's engine starting up and watches the golden stream of his headlights flow away before she walks slowly back to the desk, staring anxiously at the clock's unchanging face. She returns to the kitchen. The sight of her dress lying on the floor should shame her, but she is strangely numb. He hurt her. He did something she had never dreamed a man would do to her. He penetrated her flesh with a part of his body but he didn't make love to her, he sucked her blood. She can hardly believe it, and if it wasn't for the sinister red wounds in her wrist she might be able to convince herself she only imagined the unearthly experience. The punctures aren't bleeding, they don't hurt at all, and this worries her more than anything.

Listlessly slipping her dress back on, she makes an effort to ignore the haunting evidence he left behind on her flesh by sitting down at the desk and opening her book, but she finds it impossible to resurrect any interest in the sweet romantic plot.

Longing for the normal sound of a car rushing by outside, she picks up the phone.

It takes her a full, incredulous minute to accept the fact that there is no dial tone.

She sets the receiver back down and makes sure the line is connected to the jack in the wall, but when she checks again there is still no dial tone.

She sits staring into space.

An eternity passes before she hears the long sigh of the truck's tires outside like blood beginning to flow along the roads of her veins again. She suspects the sound is only an illusion, but it no longer matters. As the door opens and he crosses the threshold she knows their infinite hunger is all the reality she needs…

## Guilty Pleasures

**by**
**Maria Isabel Pita**

**A Magic Carpet Book**
0-9755331-5-0
$16.95 ( $21.95 Canada)

**Available August 2005**